H

D0177769

Jack Parker Comes of Age

Jack Parker, the fifteen-year-old son of the sheriff of Mayfield, does not enjoy a close and loving relationship with his father. When a vicious range war erupts in the area, Jack and his father are drawn closer when they find themselves fighting against an incursion by a band of Texan freebooters, and for a time it looks as though the youngster is destined to follow in his father's footsteps by becoming a lawman.

Jack Parker Comes of Age

Ed Roberts

A Black Horse Western

ROBERT HALE

© Ed Roberts 2019
First published in Great Britain 2019

ISBN 978-0-7198-2943-7

The Crowood Press
The Stable Block
Crowood Lane
Ramsbury
Marlborough
Wiltshire SN8 2HR

www.bhwesterns.com

Robert Hale is an imprint
of The Crowood Press

Typeset by
Derek Doyle & Associates, Shaw Heath
Printed and bound in Great Britain by
4Bind Ltd, Stevenage, SG1 2XT

CHAPTER 1

Folk hardly ever realize that the events they are taking part in at the time will, one day in the distant future, be regarded as history. This is especially so with young people, who lack any sense of perspective. Which is why it wasn't until many years after the event that Jack Parker fully appreciated the significance of the role he had played as a boy in the great Benton County Invasion of 1891. It was tolerably well known to him that he had at that time saved the lives of better than fifty men, but the wider implication of what had happened and how it related to the general scheme of things, eluded him until he was in his middle years.

In the summer of 1891, Jack Parker was living with his father Tom in the Wyoming town of Mayfield. Jack had turned fifteen almost a twelve-month previously, but was, at his father's insistence, still attending school. His mother had died so long ago that the boy could scarcely remember her. With assistance from his spinster sister, Tom Parker had endeavoured, since his wife's death, to raise his son to be a credit to him, and a fit person to take his right place in society as befitted the son of the sheriff of Benton County.

Jack Parker's passage from childhood to adolescence had been a stormy one, punctuated by innumerable clashes with his father. The boy had, over the last few years, grown sullen and rebellious against his father's authority. Matters came to a head on the evening of Tuesday, 5 July, when Jack petitioned his father yet again to be allowed to leave school. He felt it shameful to spend his days learning about such arcane subjects as trigonometry, when most all the other youngsters of his age were working at men's jobs. His father though, was in no mood to compromise. He said, 'I'm telling you, once for all, you'll stay put in that schoolroom 'til such time as I see fit to remove you, and there's an end to it.'

It was at this point that Jack made a deadly error. He muttered something under his breath which sounded, at least to his father's suspicious ears, like, 'You bastard!' Tom Parker was on his son in an instant, like some agile and ferocious cat going after a mouse. He gripped the young man by the arm and challenged him to repeat what he had just said. The boy's response was to stare mutinously back at his father, with an expression on his face which, in Tom's army days, would have been described as

6

'dumb insolence'. The two of them had reached an impasse and so the older man limited himself to cuffing Jack around the head and declaring angrily, 'Speak so to me again, boy, and just see what arrives to you, you hear what I tell you?'

So it was that later that night, when his father had left the house to attend to some official duty or other, Jack Parker rose from his bed, packed a few clothes in an old carpet bag, went downstairs to the kitchen and raided the larder for some comestibles, which he also placed in the carpet bag, and then walked out of the house with a view to running away from home and seeking his fortune in the wider world which lay beyond the town limits of Mayfield. He thought vaguely of lying about his age and enlisting in the army.

After leaving the house a half-hour before midnight, Jack walked out of town and then set off across the fields and agricultural land that surrounded Mayfield. He walked for four or five miles until he found himself in the vicinity of Agatha Roberts' farm. He was on good enough terms with Aggie and her 'husband' John, and figured that neither would mind if he were to spend the night in their barn. He was by now dog tired, and felt that he had put a fair distance between himself and his father. He would start off again right early on the morrow.

The barn, which stood no more than twenty yards from Aggie's cabin, was a rickety old structure, with many boards and planks either missing or rotted away. Because of this, Jack found that once he'd climbed the ladder into the hay-loft, he had a splendid view of the cabins and the yard which lay in front of them. He sank gratefully into the soft hay and allowed his mind to wander a little, mulling over what he knew about Agatha Roberts. He was aware of the scandalous fact that she was generally believed to be living in sin with John Baxter, but this had always seemed to Jack a matter of little import. He knew, too, that she was commonly known by the sobriquet 'Cattle Aggie', for reasons that were obscure to him.

What Jack did know about Aggie was that she invariably had time to talk to him when he came across her, and that she listened sympathetically to his problems. The two of them had connected in some strange way, when first they met, and Agatha Roberts, who had no children, and Jack Parker, who lacked a mother, had each found in the other something that was missing in their lives. Either Jack was the son she had never had, or Aggie the mother Jack had never known, or perhaps a little of both. Whatever the reason, it had not been chance alone which had directed his steps to her farm that night. He was more than half hoping to speak to Aggie the following morning, in order to solicit her counsel and advice.

Hardly had Jack Parker settled himself down into the hay, than he became aware of the drumming of hoof-beats. His first thought was that his father, in his capacity as sheriff, might have raised a posse to hunt him down and return him to his home. A moment's thought, though, told him that there would hardly have been time for such an enterprise to have been launched – he couldn't have been gone from his bed for more than a couple of hours, which was scarcely time for Mayfield's sheriff to raise the alarm, organize a band of mounted men and then reach the spot where his son was now concealed. Still, even if it wasn't his father coming to drag him home by the scruff of his neck, there was certainly a bunch of riders heading hard and fast in his direction, and Jack wondered what their urgency could be at this time of the night. He levered himself up from his bed of hay and went over to a part of the wall that was missing a number of planks. He saw at once that something unusual was happening, but what it could be, he hadn't the least notion.

The moon was full and shedding a cold, pale light on the scene. A troop of horsemen were riding down on Aggie Roberts' farm, heading, by the look of it, for the front yard, in front of the cabins. The men formed a neat and compact column as they rode down the dirt track that led to the house. Some of the riders carried flaming torches, and there looked to Jack to be fifteen or twenty of them. Something was certainly afoot. As he watched, the men cantered into the yard and then reined in,

9

turning their mounts so that they were all facing the little log cabins where Aggie and John Baxter lived. Jack had a sudden thought, that these riders meant harm to Aggie and John. Then he recognized one of the men and realized that it was absurd to suppose that this person would be mixed up in anything out of the ordinary: Mr Timothy Carter was one of the most prominent citizens in the district, and ran the Lord knew how many cattle. He spent much of his time away over in Cheyenne, but when in Mayfield he was treated as a man deserving respect. What he could be doing with a bunch of men like this in the middle of the night was something of a mystery to Jack.

It didn't take long for the purpose of this visit to Aggie Roberts to be explained, for she had evidently been awakened by either the sound of the horses or the light from the flickering torches. The front door was thrown open and she emerged, wearing a long nightgown, covered with a wrapper. Agatha Roberts was not one to mince her words, and when she spotted Carter among the men, she hailed him in a loud and fearless voice, crying, 'I'll thank you not to disturb my sleep at this ungodly hour, Timothy Carter. What's the meaning of it?'

'The meaning is that you've been dancing between the raindrops for too long Aggie, and this is the night you get caught in the storm!' called back Carter, raising a laugh from the other men.

'Care to speak a little plainer? I say again, what do

10

you mean by this?'

It was at this point that John Baxter came out of the house, also in a nightgown and with a nightcap upon his head. Truth to tell, he presented a faintly ridiculous spectacle in this get-up, and there were more chuckles at the sight of him. Baxter was a Justice of the Peace, and when dealing out the law, few people would have dared to laugh out loud at him; but there was a wild and lawless spirit abroad that night, and all the usual rules seemed to be in abeyance. Even Jack Parker, young and green as he was, could feel that this was one of those occasions when anything might happen.

Despite his undignified attire, John Baxter had lost none of the peppery manner for which he was renowned. He was in his early forties, but had an air of authority and erudition that always made him seem older than his years. He was good and mad at the scene in Agatha Roberts' yard, and made sure to let the men present there know just how he felt about this invasion of private property. Catching sight of Timothy Carter, he said angrily, 'What the devil are you about, Carter? I'll be mighty obliged if you and the rest of these scallywags remove yourself from here as soon as you like. You're trespassing.'

For a moment there was dead silence, and it seemed to Jack as though this had all been just some piece of high jinks which had, for a moment, threatened to get out of hand but was now brought under control by a few well chosen words from the

11

local Justice of the Peace. The spell was broken, though, by Carter's mocking laughter. He chuckled richly and said, 'You got a way with words Baxter, I'll allow. We all been reading your piece in the Examiner last week. Speculators and land grabbers, is it?'

'I tell it like it is. Now clear off this land or by God, I'll swear out a warrant right this minute for your arrest on a charge of threatening behaviour.'

While John Baxter and Timothy Carter had been exchanging words, Jack had observed a couple of riders slip from their horses and make their way in the shadows to the front door of the cabin. He had wondered what their aim might be, but it wasn't until Baxter, now thoroughly roused, said 'You think I'm bluffing you about the warrant? You'll see!' that Jack knew what the men were doing. After menacing the gang with issuing a warrant, John Baxter presumably decided to make good on his threat, for he turned on his heel, saying to Aggie Roberts, 'Come Agatha, leave these fools to their own devices.' and headed back inside. At which point, he found his way to the door blocked by two men with drawn pistols.

'Are you quite mad?' exclaimed Baxter, when he saw the armed men barring the way into his home, 'What damn-fool game is this? Just clear the way there, or you'll both end up in gaol.' The men stood there imperturbably, waiting for orders from Timothy Carter. These were not long in coming, for

Carter said briskly, 'You all know what we're here for. Let's get on with it!'

Now, for the first time, John Baxter showed a trace of fear. He covered this by speaking in an even sharper voice. He said, 'You men leave here this very minute and happen I'll forget the whole affair.' In reply, the men who had been blocking the way back into the house, moved forward and grabbed Baxter's arms. At the same time, another three men dismounted and moved in on Aggie Roberts. She made as if to run, but they were too quick for her. Other men got down from their mounts and one of them began looking in his saddlebag for something. With a thrill of horror, Jack saw that he was taking out first one rope, and then another.

Even now, the full significance of what he was seeing had yet to sink into Jack Parker's mind. He was still thinking in terms of some piece of mischief, a cruel and malicious prank designed to scare people, rather than cause them any real harm. Watching the unfolding scene below put him in mind of a group of bullies in the schoolyard, gaining pleasure from shoving around and tormenting a younger or weaker child. Such incidents never ended with anything worse than a few tears or bruises. There is, however, a world of difference between life in the schoolyard, which is all that Jack Parker had, up to that time, known, and the way that matters are sometimes conducted among adults.

13

A little way from the cabins was a stout oak tree. The man carrying the ropes went to this and, standing beneath it, casually formed a noose at the end of each of them. Then he swung one of the nooses round and round a few times, before sending it sailing up and over a branch. He then performed a similar trick with the second rope and looked across to Timothy Carter, as though awaiting further instructions. These were not long in coming: Carter said, 'Two o' you fellows take the end of each rope. And take these two scoundrels over to the tree.'

Both Aggie Roberts and John Baxter offered resistance, but to no avail. They were dragged and pushed inexorably towards the nooses hanging from the oak tree. When they reached it, Baxter said, in a calmer voice than he had hitherto used, 'You'll answer for this, Carter. You don't think you can get away with murder as well as all your other villainies?'

'I reckon I'll take my chance on that,' replied Timothy Carter, 'With you and your lady friend out of the way, I look to have a free run at things.'

'At least spare Aggie,' said Baxter, for the first time a note of desperation creeping into his voice, 'You can't deal so with a woman. Do what you must with me, but for the Lord's sake let her alone.'

'Not a bit of it,' said Carter, pleased to observe what he took to be a sign of weakness in the man whom he regarded as his deadly and implacable enemy. In a louder voice, he cried, 'String them up.

14

Show what happens to rustlers and cattle thieves hereabouts.'

For Jack Parker, the scene below him was like something from one of his worst nightmares, and just as sometimes happens in the course of bad dreams, he had an overwhelming desire to shout out loud, but found that he could not find his voice. All that came out of his mouth were strangled gasps and whimpers. As he watched, the two victims of the mob had their hands lashed behind their backs and the nooses were then placed around their necks. Jack had an idea that on such solemn occasions, people were generally afforded the opportunity to say a few last words, or to pray or something. In this present case, no such indulgence was offered to the doomed man and woman. No sooner were the ropes around their necks and their wrists secured, than two men each took hold of the loose ends of the ropes and began to pull, until Aggie Roberts and John Baxter were both hauled aloft.

Both of those lynched that night died hard, kicking and choking their lives out for several minutes before they lost consciousness. When it appeared to Carter that they were both dead, he directed his men to tie the ends of the ropes round the trunks of the tree, leaving the corpses dangling from the branches. Then, at another word of command, the flaming torches were tossed into the two cabins, firing them. Not until both wooden structures were blazing merrily did Timothy Carter appear to be satisfied with the night's work, and gave the order to depart.

There was, needless to say, no possibility of sleep that night for Jack Parker. Even after Carter and his men had left, he was too terrified to move from the barn and expose himself to view. It was not until the first glimmering of false dawn in the eastern sky that he bestirred himself and set off back to Mayfield. There was no question of continuing upon his chosen course, not after witnessing such a shocking crime. Whatever his feelings currently might be about his pa, Jack knew that Tom Parker was the law in Benton County, and that it would be his proper duty to make sure that these brutal deaths were avenged. The sooner that he reported the matter, the sooner that Timothy Carter and his bullies would be brought to justice.

Dawn had arrived before Jack reached the edge of town. After seeing the terrible crime that he had been compelled to witness just a few short hours earlier, the boy was vaguely surprised to find that life in the little town seemed to be proceeding much as usual. Well, he thought, all that would soon change. As soon as his father had been apprised of the matter, then no doubt a posse would be mustered and Carter taken into custody and unceremoniously thrown into the cell at the back of the sheriff's office. In this, though, Jack Parker was sadly mistaken.

Tom Parker was already up, and when Jack

entered through the kitchen door, his father turned to stare at him; anger plain in his face. 'Where the hell have you been, you young whelp?' was his greeting. 'You didn't sleep in your bed last night. What the devil are you about?'

In the usual way of things, Jack would have been trembling at such a reception, but he knew that there were greater things at stake here, and so he stood his ground and replied, 'I'll tell you later. Aggie Roberts is dead. Lynched. So's Mr Baxter.'

Jack's father stared at him, transfixed by the news. After a pause of a second or two, he said, 'What are you talking about, boy? I tell you now, this best not be some story you dreamed up to get yourself out of trouble.'

'It's no story, Pa. I seed it with my own eyes.'

Perhaps Tom saw how shaken up his son was, for he softened his tone somewhat and said, 'We'll talk later about where you been. Set there now and I'll pour you a cup of coffee. Now what's all this about Aggie?'

After he had poured out the whole tale to his father, Jack said, 'And that's the God's honest truth, sir. I saw Mr Carter with my own two eyes. He as good as murdered them, leastways he was in charge of the whole entire business. You going to arrest him?'

'I am not.'

'You're not? But I tell you I saw him. He was behind the whole thing.'

17

'No,' said Tom Parker, his face strained and white, 'You didn't see him, son. Fact is, you weren't even there.'

It was to be almost thirty years before Jack Parker fully understood the strange look that his father's face bore that morning. At the time, he thought that his father was tired and angry, but that wasn't it at all. When he was a grown man, with children of his own, Jack was living on the fourth floor of an apartment building. He carelessly left the window open and came out of the bedroom to find his five-year-old son leaning so far out that he was in serious danger of overbalancing and falling to his death. Of course, Jack had rushed over to the child and snatched him to safety, and after he had scooped up the child with one hand and closed the window with the other, he had chanced to see his face reflected in a mirror. In an instant, he was transported back to 1891, as he recollected that peculiar look he had seen on his father's face in April of that year. That strained expression did not indicate anger at all, but rather a terrible fear for the safety of a much loved child who had been in mortal danger.

But now, as no more than a callow youth, Jack Parker wholly mistook the look on his father's face, and interpreted it as being anger at Jack's meddling in something his pa wanted to be let alone. He said suddenly to his father, 'Are you in on this? Is that why you don't want me saying aught of it?'

Now anger really did come into Tom Parker's

face, and he said sharply, 'You young fool, just do as you're bid. This is nothing to do with you.'

'Yes it is, though,' cried Jack, every bit as roused as his father, 'Aggie was a good friend to me, and I won't see her murdered in such a way and nothing done about it!'

The two of them stood there, facing each other. Then Jack recalled the hideous sight of a woman he had loved and respected choking out her life at the end of a rope and the tears came to his eyes. To his utter mortification and shame, he began sobbing like a little child, and in a moment, his father's arms were around him, comforting and strong. Jack clung to his father, who stroked his head as gently as a woman, saying 'There, it's all right son. It's all right.'

After a space, Tom let go of his boy and said unexpectedly, 'Lord, the rows I used to have with my own father, God rest him. I never thought it would come to me to play that part.'

'You used to fight with your father, sir?' asked Jack, staggered at the idea of the tough and resourceful sheriff of Benton County being a rebellious youth.

'Why, yes. Those years from being a boy to becoming a man, they're never easy for anybody. I ran away, you know, things got so bad between us. Is that what you was aiming for to do?'

Jack shuffled his feet and looked down at the floor. 'I guess.'

19

'Going for a soldier, were you?'

'Something like.'

Tom Parker dismissed the subject with a brief laugh and said, 'Well then, both you and me need to mend our ways, maybe. Meantime, happen I should trust you a mite more and tell you what's what. We surely can't carry on in this way, and that's for certain sure, I can't have you suspicioning as I was complicit in Aggie Roberts' death. It isn't to be thought of for a moment. Which means a history lesson, I guess.'

Seeing the dismay that appeared on his son's countenance at the dreadful word 'history', the sheriff's lips twitched slightly and he said, 'Don't be afeared, I don't mean "history", like in the Wars of the Roses or Shakespeare. I'm talking of what's been happening in these here parts in the last few years. Pour yourself a coffee and come with me to my study.'

When the two of them were settled in the sheriff's study, which was where he kept many of his official books, papers and records, Tom Parker said to his son, 'I don't look for you to repeat anything I say in this room to another living soul. Is that plain? You'll see why, directly.' There was a long pause, as he thought how best to proceed. Knowing, as he did, the ins and outs of the situation, it wasn't easy to gauge how much of the background he would need to explore, in order to make things comprehensible. And how much of it would make sense to his

20

son; he had no idea. At length, he said, 'I guess that the current unpleasantness began just after that hard winter we had in eighty-six. You recollect the year that I made you that sledge? When the snow and ice lay on the ground for weeks at a time?'

'I remember the sledge. I was nine or ten, wasn't I?'

'You were. Well, it was all well and good for a youngster like you, playing on your sledge and throwing snowballs, but there were men for whom that winter meant starvation and ruin. And it laid the seeds for what's happened since, including the death of your friend. It was like this. . . .'

CHAPTER 2

For the first ranchers, the Wyoming Territory was something of a paradise. There was unlimited pasture and water for the taking. They let their herds of longhorns roam the range, rounding them up when needful, to brand or despatch to the slaughterhouse. All good things come to an end, though, and after the war between the states, the government in Washington began handing out parcels of land in Wyoming to more or less anybody who wanted it, with preference given to those who had fought for the Union. Each man was allocated one hundred and sixty acres, and if he farmed it for five years, then he could file claim and the land became his in perpetuity.

None of this accorded with the wishes and desires of those already rearing stock in the Wyoming Territory. The small farms that sprang up soon enclosed their fields with barbed-wire fences, and this prevented the vast herds of cattle belonging to the big ranchers from wandering freely. Worse still was the closing off of access to rivers and streams, as the banks became lined with smallholdings; the owners of which objected to hundreds of longhorns trampling over their crops to reach the water and drink. The ranchers called this state of affairs 'losing their water rights'.

Perhaps the most irksome aspect of these developments was that some of the newcomers began keeping cattle as well. The increase in supply had the effect of driving down the price, and in the mid eighteen-eighties, the price of beef plummeted. Large landowners blamed this on the settlers and homesteaders, for whom they coined a variety of unflattering epithets, such as 'squatters' and 'nesters'. There was an even worse name that the new homesteaders were called, and that was 'rustlers'. The story was put about by the big cattle barons that steers were being stolen wholesale and that the chief culprits were the nesters and squatters. Theft of cattle or horses was treated in those days with the utmost severity, and the usual consequence, if once a man were detected in the act, was summary justice, known commonly as lynching.

The winter of 1886 was so harsh that three-fourths of the cattle in Wyoming were wiped out. Following this disaster, the big ranchers reorganized how they raised their herds, relying less upon longhorns and instead introducing new, cross-bred types. That and various other innovations rejuvenated the industry, leaving only the problem of the homesteaders who were still flocking to the territory. A body called the Wyoming Stock Growers Association was founded, whose aim was to guard the interests of the rich against the paupers who were flooding in from the east. By 1891, the WSGA had become immensely rich and powerful, numbering among its members the State Governor and both senators for the new state of Wyoming. All that remained was to drive out the squatters and nesters and everything would be right in Wyoming.

'And that's pretty much how things stood until two weeks ago,' Tom Parker told his son, 'When John Baxter decided to write something about the situation for the newspapers.' He reached into a pile of papers, delved around for a bit and then pulled out a page from a newspaper, which he handed to Jack. 'Read this,' he said.

The page was from the front of the 25 June 1891 edition of The Buffalo Examiner; Incorporating the Wyoming Territory Agricultural Gazette and Intelligencer. Jack Parker read the following article, which was signed at the bottom by John Baxter:

The citizens of both Benton County and its fair neighbour Johnson County, are heartily and irredeemably sick of the activities of the speculators and land grabbers who are making the

24

lives of honest men and women a veritable misery, with their unfounded and unwarranted accusations of 'rustling' and cattle theft. The greedy and rapacious villains who hope to seize all the land in Wyoming and use it for their own purposes, are squeezing out all the settlers and homesteaders who live quietly on land legally granted to them by the Federal Government. By calumniating these decent folk as 'rustlers' and labelling them 'squatters' and 'nesters', the wealthy men who run the WYOMING STOCK GROWERS ASSOCIA-TION, including its leading light, TIMOTHY CARTER, think to turn right-minded people against their law-abiding neighbours and let the bully-boys of the W.S.G.A. ride roughshod over their ancient liberties. They need not imagine for a moment that they will be per-mitted to act in this fashion for very much longer!

'Two days after that was published,' said Tom Parker, 'somebody smashed the front window of the Examiner's office and lobbed in a stick of dynamite. Nobody was hurt, but their printing press was pretty well wrecked. These boys don't fool around when you get crosswise to them.'

'But you've got them now! I can swear in court that Timothy Carter was there when Aggie Roberts was killed, that it was his doing.'

Sheriff Parker shook his head sadly and said, 'You've a lot to learn, son. First off is that I'd have to arrest Carter and then persuade the district attorney to prosecute him. Then there'd be the grand jury indictment, and after that a trial. I'll tell you now that the district attorney will do whatever the governor tells him, and Governor Barber is a member in good standing of the Wyoming Stock Growers Association. Any jury'd be made up of property owners, men who also have a stake in things staying the way they are. Even without being threatened or bribed, they'd most likely vote to acquit. But that's not the worst of it. I don't think it would even get that far. My guess is that once word got out that there was a witness to the murder, they'd come after you, seeking your life.'

Hearing this from his father came as a dreadful shock to Jack. He was beginning to see now why his father was adamant about him keeping quiet about what he had seen. But it was all wrong, and he said to his father, 'Can't anything be done? Are they just to get away with it?'

'Not while I got breath in my body,' said Tom Parker grimly, 'But this needs careful thought. There's more than one lawman been killed by these fellows, you know.'

'You don't mean they'd kill you, Pa?'

'They might. They just might, if I gave them cause and enough ordinary folk were on their side.'

It is only in storybooks that families change

26

abruptly overnight and the members all suddenly behave differently towards each other, following some illness, injury or other reason. It would be pleasant to relate that such was the case after the conversation that Sheriff Parker and his son had that morning, but it wouldn't be true. The two of them still got on each other's nerves after the talk they had that morning, but the seeds had been sown that day of a deeper understanding on both sides. Jack still found his father overbearing and apt to throw his weight around, and for his part, Tom Parker was frequently irritated by the cavalier attitude that his son displayed towards academic achievement. But something had changed for the better in their relationship, and after the night of the two lynchings, things were never again as awkward and strained between the two of them. In later years, both of them would regard the killing of Aggie Roberts as the catalyst that ultimately brought them together, after the estrangement of adolescence.

Sheriff Parker waited until he was officially notified by another person of the deaths of John Baxter and Agatha Roberts, keeping his son's involvement in the affair a closely guarded secret. That being so, he had no legitimate excuse to approach Timothy Carter about the two deaths. There is no telling how long Jack would have been able to restrain himself from talking of his first-hand knowledge of the crime to his friends in the schoolyard, which meant that it was a mercy that the summer vacation began just two days after the news broke about the murders. Jack was looking forward with great eagerness to the summer, which he proposed to spend in fishing, hunting and other relaxing pursuits. His plans received a rude shock however, when his father announced that this year was going to be different from preceding ones. How the thing had been worked, Jack had no idea at all, although he suspected that the hidden machinations on the part of his Aunt Marion, his pa's sister, were at work.

Aunt Marion often expressed the view that boys were a trouble and that Jack especially was a young limb of Satan. It would be just like her to spoil a fellow's fun, thought Jack wrathfully, when his father told him what the summer would be holding for him this year. About this, however, he was quite wrong. The scheme was entirely of his father's devising. He had done a lot of thinking since that fateful morning, the night after his son ran away from home, and the sheriff, as a fair man, had been forced to concede that no little portion of the blame for the bad atmosphere in the house which he shared with his son attached to him, rather than the boy. He had accordingly decided that it was time to let the youngster have a taste of the real world and think matters over a little, as touching upon either going off to college at some point, or starting straight in on a job of work.

'Seems to me,' said Sheriff Parker, as he outlined

the plan to Jack, 'As you're no longer a child. Maybe I should o' noticed before, but there, there's naught to be done about what's past. We can remedy matters this year, though. Next month or so, there'll be work, not play, for you.'

At these words Jack's heart sank, for when his father spoke of 'work', Jack thought that he most likely talked of schoolwork, reading and ciphering and so on. He had known some older boys whose parents had engaged tutors for them, in preparation for college. Something of what was going through his mind must have shown on his face, for his father's eyes glinted with sudden amusement. He said, 'You can make yourself easy, if you think that you're going to be spending your days doing sums or learning about the constitution. Not but that you wouldn't benefit from such a course of action.'

'What'll I be doing then, sir?'

'How'd you like to spend some time helping your pa?'

This was such a novel idea that Jack hardly knew what to say. He temporized by saying slowly, 'I don't rightly understand what you mean.'

'Here's the way of it,' said his father, 'We're a man down at the moment. It don't matter why, that don't signify. But it means that I need somebody to do stuff for the horses, tidy up round the office, maybe write up some documents. You think you might help with it?'

'I reckon so. You mean we'd be working together?'

'Lord help me, I guess that's what I'm saying, yes. Not all the time, mind. Sometimes I need somebody to set in the office and take note of enquiries and suchlike. But I dare say we'll see much of each other, yes. What do you say?'

'I'd sure like to give it a go, sir.'

'Good boy. We'll begin Monday. Best make the most of tomorrow, for you're not apt to have a mort o' spare time after this coming sabbath.'

And so began the period of Jack Parker's life which, he later realized, marked, very sharply, the end of his childhood. Hitherto he had been protected from the realities of life by spending his days at school, with boys who were for the main part a good deal younger than he. That summer of 1891, when his father took him on as, what was to all intents and purposes, an apprentice lawman, was the time when Jack learned about how the world really worked. It was, by the by, very different from the way things had been represented to him while he was attending school and going to church and Sunday School. By the time the summer ended and he had celebrated his sixteenth birthday, Jack wondered how he could ever have been such an innocent.

The first few days of helping out his father passed peaceably enough for Sheriff Parker's son. The boy swept the floor, tidied the office, went to the livery stable to see about the care of horses, and ran errands around town for his father. It was on the Wednesday that word was received of another lynching. The death of Aggie Roberts and John Baxter had been guyed up by local ranchers as a straightforward case of a pair of rustlers getting their due deserts. Aggie had certainly kept cattle, hence the nickname of 'Cattle Aggie', and Baxter, in addition to being her lover, was also her business partner in this enterprise. Whether they had really been engaged in snatching steers from the open range and somehow spiriting them away was another matter entirely. Tom Parker did not believe it for a moment, but there were plenty in town who did. The general prosperity of the town of Mayfield was founded upon the cattle trade, and money flowed in from the big ranchers and their workers. Most of the homesteaders were as poor as Job's cat, so if there was a side to be taken in any dispute, it made sense to be with the cattle barons, rather than the two-bit sod-busters. This little piece of realpolitik was quite shocking to Jack when he learned about it from his father. It had never before struck him that decent people might be inclined to turn a blind eye to murder, just for the sake of their business interests. Still and all, that was how things were – at least according to his father, who ought to know.

Despite theoretically working together, in actual fact Jack and his father saw little of each other for most of the day. The sheriff had many things to attend to around Mayfield and in the surrounding farms, so he was seldom in the office. It was to ensure that the office was never left unattended that Tom Parker had thought it a smart dodge to have his son around the place. On Wednesday, however, the two of them were both in the office when the door was flung open and a man rushed in, saying breathlessly, 'There's been another lynching, sheriff.'

'The devil there has!' exclaimed Tom Parker, 'Where now?'

'Fellow called Carmen, had a claim up by the river.'

'Is it certain he's dead?

'Seed him with my own two eyes. Spoke to his wife, what's more. She told me he was taken.'

'Well,' said the sheriff calmly, 'If he's dead, then there's no point in hurrying. Set yourself down there and tell me the way of it. Jack, could we rustle up a pot of coffee for our visitor?'

Joe Abbot, once he was settled in a chair with a pot of strong, black coffee near at hand, related the sad story. It appeared that three men had called at Frank Carmen's home a little after dusk and represented themselves as having a warrant to take him off for questioning about the theft of a maverick. According to his wife, Frank had been dubious about the whole thing, but since the other men had him covered with drawn pistols, there was little he could do. The party set off north, in the direction of

32

the river.

Abbot had some business of an agricultural nature to conduct with Frank Carmen and so called at his cabin, early that morning. When Frank's wife told him what had happened, Abbot had ridden up the track a ways until he had come to a little clearing, where there dangled from a branch the body of Frank Carmen. A square of pasteboard had been affixed to the body and this bore, in red paint, the single word 'Thief'.

Having delivered himself of this information, Joe Abbot was in no hurry to linger in the sheriff's office. He said, 'Those boys, meaning Carter and his scamps, are running pretty free. From all I'm able to apprehend, you're no more able to stop 'em than we are, Sheriff Parker.'

Jack was shocked to hear somebody speaking to his father in this way, but Tom Parker didn't seem at all put out. He rubbed his chin and said, 'You might recollect that old saying, the one as touches upon giving a man enough rope 'til he hangs his self.'

'The only folk being hanged round these parts are innocent men and women, just trying to make an honest living,' observed Abbot, before wishing the sheriff a good day and leaving, presumably to spread the news of the latest outrage.

His father's face was thunderous at hearing this Parthian shot and so Jack said nothing, waiting to see what would happen next. His father caught sight of his nervous expression and he said at once,

'Don't take on boy, every time you see me frowning so. I ain't vexed with you.'

'So what will you do, sir?'

'Well, we'll make a start, if you can fetch three horses for us. Get them tacked up and bring them here.'

'Three? Is somebody else coming with us?'

'No, but someone else'll be returning,' said Sheriff Parker dryly, 'Less'n you fancy sharing your mount with a dead man, you'd best bring an extra horse.'

After Jack returned from the livery stable, leading the required three mounts, he and his father set off to seek the late Frank Carmen. This was the first time that his father had actually consented to allow Jack to join him on any official business and he felt a keen sense of excitement.

Before heading up to the woods which fringed the river, Tom Parker called on the widow Carmen – although she had yet to learn of the melancholy circumstance of her bereavement. Joe Abbot had not wanted to break the news and felt that the sheriff was the proper person to undertake the task. When she heard the horses approaching, Mary Carmen rushed from her home and, recognizing the sheriff, cried, 'Thank God you're here. Is there any news of my husband? I'm guessing Joe told you what's afoot?'

The sheriff said, 'Joe Abbot came by my office this day, yes. Told me that your husband was taken last night.'

'Said they had a warrant,' said Mary Carmen, 'Didn't look much like lawmen, though.'

'Well,' said the sheriff, 'Me and my assistant here, we're going up by the river to see what's what. That's the way they went, yes?'

'You'll come and tell me directly if you find aught, yes?'

'That I will, Mrs Carmen, that I will.'

They set off downhill. If Mary Carmen had guessed the reason for the third horse which they were leading, she had given no indication of it.

It wasn't hard to find the clearing of which Abbot had told them; it was right on the path. The hanging body put Jack Parker in mind of the death of Aggie Roberts and he gulped, fighting back tears. His father, though, walked his horse forward and then dismounted; following which he walked around the corpse, examining it from all angles. Jack too got down from his horse, but felt unable to approach the hanged man. Instead, he looked around the glen and spied something lying by a tree-root. He went across and bent down to pick the thing up. It was a half-smoked cigarillo. Holding it up to his ear, he rolled it back and forth a little, listening to the dry rustling of the leaves from which it had been made. Then his father called irritably, 'Are you going to stop fooling around over there, for I could surely do with a hand here.'

Popping the cheroot into his pocket, Jack went

over to help his father cut down the body of Frank Carmen. At first, he shrank back from the feel of the dead flesh, but his father said, 'What's wrong with you? You're more delicate than a girl.' So he held the corpse steady, as Sheriff Parker sawed away at the rope. He had to mount his horse in order to gain enough height to reach the taut rope above the noose which encircled Carmen's neck. He said to his son, 'Take a hold of him now, I don't want to see him tumble into the dust like a piece of trash. He deserves respect, even in death.'

After a second or two, the rope parted and jack Parker found himself in the disagreeable position of more or less embracing a corpse. He endeavoured at first to hold the man upright, but this proved impossible and so he gently lowered the late farmer into a sitting position. Something which struck the boy most forcibly was that in cheap thrillers, the sort of novelettes and dime novels which were almost all he ever read, dead bodies are sometimes carried by people who pretend that they are merely drunk; so that they can get out of a scrape of some kind. They might smuggle the corpse past a lawman by gripping its arms and saying, 'Come on fellow, you had too much to drink, you know!' This real dead body, though, was nothing like a drunk man. There was something indefinably awful about a corpse, which could never be mistaken for anything else. This stuck in Jack's mind for many years afterwards – the dead feel of the body.

Once the two of them had laid the body carefully, and with as much dignity as was possible, over the saddle of the spare mount, lashing the ankles to the wrists so that it would not slide off, the two of them stopped for breath. Tom Parker said to his son, 'We'd best take a look around, but I'm not hopeful of finding anything to tie this foul business to anybody in especial.'

Jack took the cigarillo from his pocket and said diffidently, 'Well sir, there's this.'

His father's eyes narrowed and he took the rolled leaves from Jack. He said, 'This might've lain here a good long while. There's no way o' knowin' if it was smoked by one of them as did this thing.'

Very hesitantly, Jack said, 'Well, I figure that it was raining pretty hard, late yesterday afternoon, up 'til dusk. If this had been laying here then, it would be soggy and wet now. But just listen to it, when you roll it. It's dry as a bone. I reckon somebody dashed it down last night, after the rain stopped.'

The sheriff held the cheroot up to his ear and did as his son had suggested. Then he sniffed it delicately, as though he were smelling some fragrant rose. Giving his son an odd and inscrutable look, he said, 'You're something else again, son. You know that?'

'Have I done something wrong?' asked the boy anxiously.

'You done something right is more how I would put it. I should have looked round here a bit myself

37

before troubling myself about a man who was already dead.' Tom Parker handed the cigarillo to his son and said, 'Here, smell this.'

After sniffing dubiously, Jack said, 'That's strange. It smells a bit like candy.'

'Don't it though? It's aniseed. They flavour the leaves with it sometimes, it's popular down south in Mexico. You get it in Texas too, just across the border.'

'Does it signify?'

'It might. Timothy Carter has a couple of Texans working on his spread. It's what I told Joe Abbot this morning. Give a man enough rope and he's certain-sure to hang himself in the end. Good work, son. For spotting this, I mean.'

In all his days, Jack Parker had never heard any-thing as dreadful and spine-chilling as the shriek that Mary Carmen emitted, when she caught sight of her dead husband. Perhaps she had been waiting for them to return from the river, because Mrs Carmen was outside her cabin and there was no way of avoid-ing her seeing them pass by. After that initial scream, the woman set up a keening cry, which put Jack in mind of a wounded animal, caught in a trap. His father, who must have encountered such scenes before, dealt humanely but firmly with the dis-tracted widow, explaining that he needed to take the mortal remains of Frank Carmen to town, in the hope that examination of the body would yield some clue as to the perpetrators of the lynching.

Jack and his father did not speak again, not until they reached Mayfield. Both, in their different ways, were shaken by the morning's events. As they rode down Main Street with their grim burden, people on the sidewalk stopped to stare. It could only be supposed that Joe Abbot had already spread word of what had occurred, for nobody came up and asked whose body this was, or what had happened to him. It looked like they already knew.

The sheriff and his son placed the dead man in the presently unoccupied cell at back of the office. Then they washed their hands and Jack set a pot of coffee to boil. His father said, 'This is what being a lawman is really like, Jack. It's a dirty business, and you have to try and stay clean. I don't mean physically, you understand.'

'I think I see what you mean, sir.'

'Do you though? I'd think as you'd a sight rather go off to college than get mixed up in this kind of thing day by day.'

'I don't know,' replied his son slowly, 'Seems to me that you are all that stands between and betwixt a whole heap o' beastliness. You're a-guarding the folk hereabouts, even if they don't really know it.'

Sheriff Parker looked penetratingly at his boy and, after a space, said, 'I reckon you just about summed it up. You think you'd care to lend a hand at this work when you're a bit older?'

'It may be so, Pa.'

Theoretically, Sheriff Parker had two deputies.

One of them had been granted leave of absence to deal with a family loss over in Johnson County, which accounts for why the sheriff had wanted another pair of hands about the office for a week or two. The other deputy, a young man by the name of Brandon Ross, spent much of his time patrolling the areas where the homesteaders lived, reassuring them that the law would protect them. While the sheriff and his son supped their coffee, Brandon came through the door and Tom Parker gave him the bare bones of recent developments. The young man shook his head and said, 'There's already two families of settlers getting ready to dig up and leave. They say they've had enough. That Aggie Roberts business has spooked folks and no mistake, and I can't say as I blame them none. A woman hanged from a tree! I never heard the like.'

'It won't take much more,' said the sheriff, 'To trigger a regular exodus. But there's another side to the thing. People in town are disgusted about the lynchings, too. For all that the boys from the WSGA are good for trade and prosperity, nobody likes to see wanton killings like that. I'm hopeful that the mood is changing and that the folk in town might make common cause with the newcomers.'

'You reckon so?' asked Brandon Carter doubtfully.

'I'm hopeful of it. It won't take much more to tip the balance.'

Sheriff Parker's remarks on this subject proved

prescient, for the very next day an incident took place which did indeed serve to turn the tide of public opinion against Timothy Carter and his bullies. It would perhaps be more accurate to say that the following day's events were the turning point; it was to be another ten days before the town was effectually roused and prepared to stand behind their sheriff in resisting the actions of the ranchers.

CHAPTER 3

The day after he had helped bring the corpse of the late Frank Carmen to town, Jack was taking things easy at the livery stable. One of the fellows from school, a boy a year younger than him, had acquired work at the livery stable over the summer. It was pleasant to relax a little and chat with somebody more of his own age, rather than being party to grim conversations about murder, mayhem and rapine.

It was late afternoon and Jack was hopeful of his father dismissing him soon and telling him that he might go over to his Aunt Marion's for a meal. The one thing which he had not fully appreciated before coming to work with his father, was the fact that the sheriff's job was really twenty-four hours a day. He had always known that his father was out all day and often in the evening as well, but he had not really given any thought to what this actually meant. Now, he could see all the demands made upon his father's time. Only a small part of the work entailed actually detecting or preventing crime. There were permits to be issued, documents filed, land deeds examined and a hundred and one other things. The duties were wide-ranging, and related every bit as much to civil matters as they did to keeping the peace.

Jack and Pete Hedstrom were playing pitch and toss against a wall, with a few odd cents they had between them. Jack was having the best of it, when there came the sound of furious and hard riding and a man on horseback passed them at breakneck speed, heading down the street towards the sheriff's office. Some instinct told Jack that this was urgent business and he said to Pete, 'I'd best be off. That looks like it might involve my pa.'

'I never thought you got along too well with your pa,' said Pete, 'Something change between you and him?'

'Not exactly. Maybe I'm seeing another side to him lately.'

'I sure wish I could spend my time in the sheriff's office, rather than this old stable. It must be right exciting.'

'Not really that,' said Jack thoughtfully, 'Exciting isn't the word. It's important. For everybody.'

Having taken leave of his friend, Jack headed towards his father's office and was not in the slightest degree surprised to see the horse which lately he had seen being ridden so hard, tethered to the

43

hitching rail outside the office. He slipped in quietly and listened to what was being said. His father was speaking in the slow, patient tone he used when he was trying to get something important fixed clearly in his mind. He said to the man who had ridden into town, 'You're sure about that? That it's Harker, I mean?'

'Well, he's laying dead outside m'cabin. Come and see for your own self.'

'I purpose to take just such a course, but I needs must know the facts first. You kill a man, you put your neck in hazard, you know that as well as I do.'

'You think if I'd o' killed him other than in defence of myself, I would have come racing here to report the matter to you, Sheriff? Sides which, my partner's up there waiting for us. He'll take oath that what I say is the way of it.'

'I'm not questioning your word, just making sure you realize what a serious business this is.'

What had happened, as Jack later gathered from his father, was as follows. The man who had come galloping into town was a homesteader who was strongly suspected by the sheriff of moonshining. At any rate, he shared his cabin not with a wife, but another man. There was no suggestion that there was anything unnatural about this arrangement, it being widely supposed that this other fellow was by way of being a business partner in the distilling of ardent spirits. Sheriff Parker suspected that the reason that only one of the men had come to report the death was that the other was busily engaged in covering up all traces of the still and any evidence of moonshine liquor.

The two men had been sitting in their cabin when there had been a rap on the door. When they went to investigate, they found three men standing outside. They recognized Thad Harker, who was trail boss up at Timothy Carter's place. Harker had a rifle under his arm and said that it was time for the two men to be moving on, that nobody wanted any unpleasantness, but the land was to be returned to a state of nature. At first they laughed at this, for neither Ed Summerfield nor his friend were men who took kindly to folk trying to bluster them. There was a little shoving and cursing, and then Harker had seemingly cocked his piece and let off a single shot; whereupon Summerfield pulled his pistol and shot the trail boss through the heart. The dead man's accomplices then cut and ran.

If matters were as represented by Summerfield, then it was a clear case of self-defence. If somebody starts shooting, then his blood is upon his own head if somebody then puts a bullet in him. Sheriff Parker had no cause to doubt the account as it had been given, but he wished to see for himself. He was sure in his own mind that Summerfield and his partner were distilling liquor, but he didn't have them pegged for killers.

Eager as he was to come and view the scene of the shooting, Jack was instead instructed to stay behind and tend to the office in his father's absence. 'This is a serious business,' Tom Parker told him, 'Matters are coming to a head and I dare not leave the office empty if it can be helped. Besides which, men sometimes take it into their heads to exact revenge in a case of this sort. I surely wouldn't want you nearby if shooting starts.' Although he had been excited at the idea of visiting the scene of a recent shooting, Jack knew that his father was right; somebody needed to stay and look after the shop.

It was coming on towards seven when his father returned; by which time Jack's stomach was making protesting noises, he not having eaten since midday. There had been a steady stream of people wanting something or other. Sometimes it was information, some of which Jack was able to furnish them with. Others had complaints and problems which only the sheriff would be able to deal with. The folk in town were amused to find Tom Parker's boy tending the office, like he was a deputy or something. The sheriff was well liked in Mayfield, and most of them thought that he was training up his son to follow in his footsteps. If so, then that was all right with them.

Tom Parker arrived back at the office at almost precisely the same moment as his deputy. When he was settled behind his desk, the sheriff said, 'Brandon, we've a visit to pay. This has got to stop right now, or me and those fellows running the Wyoming Stock Growers Association are apt to fall out.' He glanced across at his son and said, 'You

46

want to come too? You've a crow of your own to pluck with Timothy Carter.' Brandon didn't ask what this meant, guessing that it was a private matter. The sheriff said, 'We need to eat afore we ride up there though. I'm nigh on fainting for want of vittles.'

After the three of them had snatched a hasty meal at a nearby eating house, Jack went off to tack up a horse for himself. His feelings about the projected expedition were jumbled and confused. On the one hand, it was surely exciting to be riding alongside the sheriff on such an important piece of work. On the other though, he couldn't imagine what it would be like to see Timothy Carter again. The thought made him feel a little queasy, and he hoped he would be able to conceal whatever emotions were stirred up by the sight of the man.

On the way to Carter's ranch, Sheriff Parker told the two others what had happened up at Ed Summerfield's place. Just as claimed, there lay Thad Harker, stone dead with a ball through his heart. 'It looks like a true bill to me. All that I saw tied in with what Summerfield told me. His partner backed it up as well. Mind, they're a rare pair of scoundrels. For all that they'd done their best to tidy up things, I could smell the poteen from a quarter-mile away. I read them the riot act and I hope they'll heed my advice.'

Brandon said, 'What will you say to Carter?'

'I'll ask him to stop all this foolishness of trying to

drive men off their land. I've about had enough of it, and if things go any further, we'll have a little war on our hands and I don't mean to have it so, not while I'm sheriff in Benton County.'

The land actually owned by Timothy Carter was not extensive: it amounted to no more than three hundred acres. It was the open range that surrounded his ranch which made his cattle profitable. Were he ever forced to keep them penned in on his ranch and obliged to supply them with water and hay every day, he would soon be out of business. From that point of view, one could see why he was so eager to see the back of the settlers who were engaged in closing off the range with their barbed-wire fences and stopping his steers from reaching the water they needed.

Timothy Carter lived in an imposing, stone-built house, as befitted a man of such importance. When Sheriff Parker rode up to it, accompanied by his deputy and son, Carter was standing outside, chatting to a small group of men. He recognized Tom Parker at once and greeted him affably, but with a lazy and mocking air, saying, 'Sheriff, to what do I owe the pleasure of this visit? Or is it just a social call?'

The sheriff dismounted and his deputy did likewise. Jack, unsure of his status here, remained in the saddle. He could barely bring himself to look at Timothy Carter, knowing as he did that the man was a murderer. He was afraid that something would show in his face if he looked straight at the man, and that by some means, the other would guess that Jack knew what he had done the week before.

Carter said, 'I'm glad that you came by, Sheriff. It gives me a chance to introduce you to my new man. Well, I say mine, but he's employed by the Wyoming Stock Growers Association. With all the rustling going on hereabouts, and the law unable to protect us from the scourge, we've engaged the services of Mr Booker here to hunt down those responsible. He's our range detective. Booker, I'd like you to meet our local lawman, Mr Jackson.' Booker, an ill-favoured man of about forty stepped forward and extended his hand to the sheriff. Tom Parker ignored the outstretched hand, staring coldly at the owner. Carter said, 'Dave Booker here is in the same line of work as you, Sheriff. For a spell, he was a sheriff over in Colorado.'

'And before that, bounty hunter, road agent and mercenary in Mexico,' said Sheriff Parker. 'I'm well acquainted with this man's background. Question is, what's he doing here in Benton County?' He continued to stare at Dave Booker, who met the sheriff's gaze unflinchingly, his lips faintly curled as though he found the other man a little amusing.

'Like I said,' replied Carter, 'Mr Booker is a range detective. The regular law can't seem to touch those wretches who are taking our stock and so we must fall back on the services of men like Booker.'

Dave Booker reached into his pocket and

extracted a silver case, from which he took a dark brown cigarillo, which he lit with a lucifer. Even up on his horse and some distance away, Jack caught a sweet and faintly fragrant scent. His father said pleasantly, 'That's a rare thing in these parts, Booker. Your smoke is mixed with aniseed.'

'What of it?'

'Nothing at all, just that it's not common hereabouts. You're Texan aren't you?'

'So?'

'Lord a mercy,' said Tom Parker in a good humoured way, 'But you're a touchy one! I only ever knew Texans and Mexicans to favour such smokes, that's all.' He turned to Timothy Carter and said, 'Well this isn't business. I didn't come here for idle chit-chat. There's been a tragic death. One of your men.'

'Oh?' said Carter, noncommittally.

'Your trail boss, Thadeus Harker. He died in a shooting a few hours since.'

'Thank you for notifying me, sheriff. I hope that his assassin has been apprehended?'

'Well, it appears to be as plain an instance of self-defence as you could hope to find. There aren't likely to be any arrests for it. I don't suppose that you know what he might have been up to, up by Ed Summerfield's place today?'

'I couldn't say,' said Carter, not bothering to disguise either his amusement or frank contempt for the sheriff, 'I don't follow my men about all day to see what they're about.'

'I see. Thank you, that's much as I expected.'

Timothy Carter, Dave Booker and the other half dozen men waited to hear if there was anything more that the sheriff wished to say. He duly obliged them by saying loudly, 'I want all you men to attend to what I say. There's been enough killing of late. This is the fourth violent death in a week. Well, it stops right this minute. Were I you Mr Carter, I'd call my men off and stop all these games. If you don't, then things are like to get ugly and it will be upon your own head. And you, Booker. I know what sort of man you are, and I tell you straight, I'm setting a watch on you. Set a foot wrong and I'll have you locked up in next to no time. Is that all understood?'

Nobody answered him and so the sheriff turned on his heel and mounted up again. Brandon followed suit. Timothy Carter said quietly, 'Two men and a green boy. That what you think it'll take to try conclusions with me? Well, let's see what we see.'

Without deigning to reply to this, Sheriff Parker urged on his horse and the three of them rode off.

When they were clear of the house, Tom Parker said, 'That was worthwhile, at any rate.'

'How so?', said the deputy, 'I don't see what use we've been. They'll keep up their games, for a bet.'

'Of course they will,' agreed his boss, with a grim smile on his face, 'But now we know what the game is more clearly.'

51

'Do we?' asked Jack, 'Nobody said anything!'

'Well, we know who was responsible for stringing up Frank Carmen, for one thing.' This had to be explained to Brandon, who had not heard about the finding of the unusual cheroot at the scene of Carmen's hanging. When he had been told, he observed, 'Well, I don't see that that gets us any further forward. So we know who committed a murder, we got no real evidence. You wouldn't get a jury to hang a man because of some fancy cigar.'

'*We* know who's involved,' explained the sheriff patiently, 'That counts for something. I know of Dave Booker. He's a black-hearted killer if ever there was one. Sheriff in Colorado indeed! The things that man was up to there, during the six weeks he was a peace officer, it's a miracle he wasn't hanged himself. No matter. We know where we stand now.'

'Where to now, Sheriff?' asked Brandon Ross. 'Is that it for the day?'

'Not quite. We can't leave that body up at Summerfield's cabin. They've a couple of spare horses up there, I'll borrow one and bring Harker to town. If Timothy Carter wants the corpse of his trail boss, then he can come and fetch it.'

The moonshiners' cabin was only a mile or so off their way and Tom Parker was aiming to make the slight detour, collect the body of the late trail boss and then go straight back to town. He was uneasily aware that his son had been working a long day and wanted the boy to have a bit of rest before dusk. It was not to be. As they approached the vicinity of Summerfield's home, which was nestled among the trees, shots rang out; first one or two, and then a veritable fusillade of firing. Tom Parker turned to his son and said, 'Stay here. Don't you move from this spot.' Then he and Ross spurred on their horses and galloped towards the sound of the firing, which was not slackening off.

Jack hardly knew what to do. On the one hand, he had a tremendous desire to follow his father and see what was going on. Set against this was a fear of being injured or killed. There was also the fact that if his father told him to stay put, then that was what he expected. Jack treasured the new and more cordial relationship that seemed to be developing with his father, and had no wish to hazard it by an act of pointless disobedience. It was while he was musing along these lines that the youngster came closer to death than he ever would again in the whole course of his life.

Jack was seated on his horse, athwart of the track leading to the trees. Suddenly, a rider emerged from the trees at a smart canter, heading straight in Jack's direction. Now whether or not this man thought that Jack was holding the road against him or perhaps because he was just in the mood for killing, the rider drew his pistol without slackening pace at all and without any hesitation fired twice at the boy seated peaceably on his mount. The first ball flew so close to his head that Jack heard it droning by his ear like an angry bee. The second ball struck Jack's horse, which immediately whinnied and reared up, throwing Jack to the ground.

The man who had tried to kill him did not halt to check whether or not he had accomplished his purpose; he just kept on riding as fast as he was able. The boy lay on the ground, winded from the fall. He tentatively began flexing his hands and wriggling his toes, to see if the fall had effected some mischief, but from all that he was able to collect, his body was functioning as well as it always did. The horse, though, had collapsed, narrowly missing Jack, and was now making pitiful noises, suggestive of pain and distress.

It could only have been a few seconds later that Tom Parker came racing from the trees, followed closely by his deputy. Presumably he was in hot pursuit of the man who had tried to kill Jack, but all that was forgotten in an instant when he caught sight of his son lying next to the wounded beast. The sheriff scarcely waited for his mount to come to a complete halt, before leaping from the saddle and hurrying over to where his son lay, still winded and not inclined yet to get to his feet. 'Are you hit, son?'

'No, the ball missed me. It come close though.'

'You hurt at all?'

The look of tender solicitude on his father's face was something he could never have imagined. Tom Parker looked down at his boy with such anxiety and love, that Jack almost felt that it had been worth taking a tumble, just to see his father's expression. He said, 'I'm fine, Pa. It just knocked my breath out, falling so.'

'Just stay there for a while.'

Brandon Ross said, 'We going after that fellow or not?'

'I'm going nowhere, leastways, not 'til I tended to my son. You want to take him alone, go right ahead.'

But it appeared that the deputy had no particular desire to go haring off after a ruthless killer and instead helped the sheriff to take care of the situation there. He said, 'That horse is suffering. Shall I put it out of its misery?'

Receiving no reply, his boss was too preoccupied with his son, Brandon drew his pistol and went over to the poor creature. He soothed the terrified animal, stroking its head and saying softly, 'There, there. Don't take on. It'll be all right.' While he spoke these soothing words, he brought up the barrel of the pistol and pointed it directly into the horse's ear. Then he squeezed the trigger. The beast gave one great convulsive shudder and then lay still.

It appeared that apart from being a little shaken up and probably pretty bruised, Jack had suffered no real injury from the episode. He felt wobbly on his feet when he stood, though less from the effects of crashing to the ground, and more from the dawning realization that he had come within a hair's breadth of being killed just a few minutes earlier. To take his mind off this awful thought, he asked his father what they had found when they reached the location of the shooting.

'Well, there'll be a deal less moonshine being sold hereabouts.' said the sheriff, before deciding that this flippant approach to the incident wasn't altogether fitting when talking to a youngster of such years. He said in a changed tone, 'Ed Summerfield and his friend are dead. I'm not sure how it was done, but as we arrived, a couple of men made off through the trees. Another of 'em came this way and that was the one we chose to go after.'

It was a sombre party who made their way back to Mayfield. There were now three corpses to transport back to town, but Sheriff Parker was frankly uninterested in this task, being more concerned with getting his son back and safely tucked up in his bed. It was twilight, and if they weren't swift about it, they would lose the light. Jack was placed on one of the horses tethered near Summerfield's cabin and the three of them proceeded at a gentle trot, with his father constantly asking if the boy was feeling all right or wished to stop for a rest.

As soon as they got back to town, before even going to his office, the sheriff delivered Jack to the care of his sister. Aunt Marion could be a real fussbudget at times, but right now Jack was grateful for her attentions. She sat him down and applied arnica to his bruises, before preparing a bowl of broth for him. His father took leave of them and promised to return as soon as he had dealt with the paperwork for the day's events.

The circumstance of Jack almost being killed had affected both father and son very greatly, and served to cement the new understanding which had existed between them since the murder of Aggie Roberts and John Baxter. For his part, Jack recalled the look on his father's face when he feared that his son had been badly injured, and was assured that however much he might conceal his emotions in the usual way of things, his father loved him fiercely. He would do anything at all now for his father, having received this reassurance of how precious he was to him.

It wasn't short of half past ten before Tom Parker returned to take Jack home. Aunt Marion had insisted that the boy sit quietly after he had finished his broth, and she tried to get him to relax a little by reading to him from one of Charles Dickens' books. Doubtless it was kindly meant, but of all things in the world, Jack could imagine nothing less relaxing than to be compelled to listen to Dickens' description of a case in the Chancery division of the London courts. He resolved that if he lived to be a hundred, he would never trouble himself to read *Bleak House*.

After the dramatic events that had taken place over the course of a week or so, most people had the feeling that matters were drawing swiftly towards a bloody climax. Just exactly as Sheriff Parker had predicted, the mood in Mayfield was changing, and it wasn't swinging round in favour of the new homesteaders, but more plumb against Carter and the men of the WSGA. It would have been one thing if matters were showing any sign of settling down a little and getting back to normal, but that was very far from how it was currently looking. Few people believed that the range was truly infested with rustlers and cattle thieves in the way that Timothy Carter was representing the situation. It was rather becoming plain that mercantile considerations alone lay behind the spate of recent murders, and this did not sit well with the town. If a man would organize killings simply because somebody was costing him money or threatening his profit margin, then where would it end? Would Timothy Carter and his men be prepared to deal so ruthlessly with the citizens of Mayfield itself, should they get crosswise to his plans?

Tom Parker went about his business during the next few days without trying to get folk stirred up against Carter and the other big ranchers. He believed, quite correctly, that the deaths of the settlers was acting like yeast on the town, slowly fermenting and causing a sea-change in attitudes.

During this quiet spell, which subsequent events showed to have been the lull before the storm, the sheriff gave more thought to his son than he had since the boy was a babe in arms. He knew that he had come within a whisker of losing the most precious thing in his life, and he did not aim to see Jack set in hazard again. He said to the boy the day after the shooting of Ed Summerfield, 'You got the rest of the summer to yourself, son. You can fish, hunt, do whatever you want. I'm mighty obliged to you for the help in the office, but things are quieter now. Maybe next summer we can fix up a similar arrangement?'

But Jack would by no means consent to this plan, telling his father, 'That won't answer, Pa.' He said this not in a petulant or sulky way, but straight and true; looking his father in the eye.

'Won't answer, hey? I'd like to know why the devil not.'

His son reasoned the case out so clearly that the sheriff was a little staggered. 'First off,' said Jack, 'is where you still need somebody else in the office. I see what you been contending with there. Brandon Ross is a good fellow, but he can hardly write a word without consulting the dictionary.'

At this, Sheriff Parker laughed out loud. 'So all those years in school have been some use to you, after all. What more?'

'I can shoot as well as you with a rifle. Better, maybe.' This was indisputably true, and it was generally acknowledged that young Jack Parker was one of the best shots in the area. He had won the prize for marksmanship at the last County Fair. Before his father could respond to this, Jack went on, 'Aggie

Roberts stood friend to me. I saw her killed. I can't forget her, I have to help bring that damned villain to book.'

'Watch your language,' said Tom Parker automatically. He continued, 'You ain't about to give up on this, are you? Not even if I beg you to reconsider?'

'I can't, Pa. It's like a duty.'

His father sighed and said finally, 'Well then, I guess we'll have to have it so. At least take today and tomorrow off and see your friends. You can come to the office again on Friday. That suit?'

'Yes sir, Thank you. I don't mean to be contrary. . . .'

His father did a thing which he had not done for some years. He reached forward and ruffled Jack's hair. Then he bent forward and kissed his son on the top of his head. Without another word, he left the room.

CHAPTER 4

That day and the one after, Jack Parker fooled around with his friends. But although this was how he had always loved to spend his summers, now he felt that something was lacking. He was unable to put his finger on precisely what that might be, but somehow haring around the fields and talking about fishing and what would happen at school in September, seemed to have lost its flavour. The youngster was wondering more about the activities of the WSGA and trying to figure out what the next step in their game would be.

Jack had still not related to anybody the circumstance which led to his witnessing the murder of Aggie Roberts and John Baxter, and nor, surprisingly, did he feel in any way impelled to talk of the close shave he had had when somebody took a shot at him. He knew instinctively that something like this, which had happened in the course of law enforcement, was not the kind of thing one bandied around in casual conversation. His friends, for their part, sensed a new reserve in Jack. It was most noticeable when conversation turned to the shortcomings of their parents, a favourite topic among the boys at the school. Jack, who had always been among the most vociferous critics of male parents in general and his own in particular, was now silent on the subject. Nor would he be drawn into the discussion at all and this, after a while, made the other boys a little uneasy and they stopped talking of their own fathers' tyrannical behaviour. All in all, the two days that he spent with his friends were stale and flat, compared with the days spent working with his father.

On Thursday morning, Jack went with his father to the office. Something he marked was that as the two of them walked through the streets now, people no longer grinned or made light-hearted remarks to the effect that Sheriff Parker had got himself a new deputy. Instead, they nodded soberly to the sheriff and included Jack in the greeting. Somehow or other, perhaps via Brandon Ross chatting unguardedly in some saloon, word had got about of the fact that Tom Parker's son had been under fire. He was changing in the minds of the town's folk from schoolboy to young man.

When they reached the office, Brandon was already there and he handed the sheriff a telegram, saying, 'You best read that, boss.' Tom Parker studied the thing and then, without thinking, passed it to his son. It read as follows:

PARIS TEXAS. REPRESENTATIVES OF WSGA IN TOWN AND HIRING MEN STOP CLAIM TO BE CLEARING PART OF WYOMING OF RUSTLERS AND STOCK THIEVES STOP MORE THAN FIFTY MEN ENGAGED STOP GOOD WAGES AND TRAIN HAS BEEN HIRED TO TAKE THEM NORTH NEXT WEEK STOP LOOKS MORE LIKE ARMY OF BUSHWHACKERS THAN RANGE DETECTIVES STOP LIKELY TO ARRIVE CHEYENNE TEN DAYS FROM PRESENT DATE STOP REGARDS MAR-SHALS OFFICE PARIS.

'This has been sent to all county seats in the state,' said Brandon, 'You think it specially affects us?'

'I reckon so,' said the sheriff, 'Texas, hey? You think it's just happenstance that Carter's new "range detective" is from down that way? I don't think it for a moment.'

'What should we do?' asked the deputy. To his amazement, Sheriff Parker turned to his son and said,

'What do you say, Jack? What would you do if you was in charge?'

Jack was almost as astonished as Brandon Ross was to find his opinion being solicited in this way. He thought for a second and then said slowly, 'I'd make sure that they told me in Cheyenne when this train gets in and see if anybody there could say which way the men were heading.'

His father nodded approvingly and said, 'Anything more?'

'Yes,' said Jack with growing confidence, 'I'd work on the notion that they're heading for us. I'd start finding which men would be ready to join us in putting a stop to it.' He realized that both Brandon Ross and his father were staring at him and Jack flushed like a schoolgirl, ending by mumbling, 'Anyways, that's how it seems to me would be the way of it.'

'What about you, Brandon?' asked Tom Parker, 'Let's have your views and opinions on the question.'

'Pretty much the same as your boy, I guess.'

'Well, that makes it easy enough, if we're all agreed on the course of action. Brandon, wire Cheyenne and get them to set a watch for these rogues. And Jack, you can come with me. We'll sound out a few folks this very morning.'

When they were clear of the office and walking down main street, Tom Parker asked his son abruptly, 'How would you feel about carrying that rifle of yours along of you for a while?'

'What, you mean in town and all?'

'Well, you're no sort of use with a pistol, that's for sure. I'd feel easier in my mind if you were carrying something, you understand me?'

Jack turned over this proposal for a bit and then

said, 'Wouldn't people think it was odd, seeing me with a gun all the time?'

'How so? A lot of folks go heeled all the time. Not as many as once did, I'll grant you, but it's still not uncommon.'

'You want I should go home and fetch it now?

'No, tomorrow will do.'

The first place that the sheriff and his son visited was the mayor's residence. If any concerted attempt was to be made to oppose the men who were evidently heading their way from Texas, then the mayor's support would be vital. Mayor Collins was at home that morning and as amenable as could be. 'You want to raise a posse, sheriff? Of course, you know best. You don't need my say-so, you know.'

'It's not your say-so I want, Mayor,' said the sheriff. Bill Collins was a regular stickler for protocol, and even in his private capacity, preferred people to address him as 'Mayor Collins', rather than Collins or even Bill. People would take their lead from him, though, and there was no legal compulsion for anybody to sign up to ride with a posse. Sheriff Parker continued, 'What it is, Mayor, is that a word from you would show people where their rightful duty lay. When the time comes, will you advise people that there's an emergency and that they should ride against these boys from Texas?'

This direct question put Mayor Collins in a tricky position and he did not wish to commit himself as being either for or against the project. On the one hand, he enjoyed excellent relations with the men from the Wyoming Stock Growers Association and there was no doubt that they were good for Mayfield, looked at in a purely financial light. On the other hand, having folk murdered near the town was not at all the sort of thing that anybody wished to see. And Collins had no doubt, any more than the sheriff did, that if once a band of fifty Texan cut-throats fetched up in the neighbour-hood, then the previous deaths would most likely be multiplied a hundredfold. In the end, he decided to procrastinate, as he so often did when a difficult problem presented itself. He said to Sheriff Parker, 'Tell you what, why don't we see first if these fellows really are heading this way? Happen they'll be going not here but to Johnson County or somewhere. If so, the law there'll take care of 'em.'

As he and Jack left, the sheriff turned at the door and, dropping any pretence at formality, said bluntly, 'Sooner or later, Bill, you'll have to come down on one side or the other.'

Elsewhere, at the saloon, in the stores, and even at one of Mayfield's churches, the response was more promising. It was looking as though many people could see which way the wind was blowing and were not at all happy about the recent turn of events. Half a dozen men allowed that things were not looking good and that if push came to shove, then they would like as not stand behind Sheriff Parker. There was no great enthusiasm for the idea of going up against a bunch of gunmen from out of state, but the alternative would be to surrender law and order entirely to outsiders.

A little after midday, Tom Parker said to his son, 'You can cut along now, boy.'

'You don't need me any more today?'

'I want you to take that gun of yours out and get a little practice. I don't much mind what you fire at, but you need to be on good form for a while.'

Jack looked at his father a little nervously and said, 'You don't think anybody would shoot at me, sir?'

His father thought for a bit before answering and then said, 'I don't think it, but there's no saying that somebody might not take a shot at me. Hell, I suppose that if somebody wished to harm me, they might hit upon the notion of hurting you; which would be a grief to me. While things are uncertain, I'd sooner know that you were armed than not.'

Jack needed no second bidding, but went straight home and took his beloved rifle from the closet in which it rested, along with a scattergun, a weapon Jack had never really taken to. The rifle was an 1866 Winchester, the model with the brass receiver which had earned it the nickname of 'Yellow Boy'. The magazine held fifteen rounds. The rimfire cartridges it used were not always easy to obtain, more modern firearms favouring centre-fire, but Jack adored the rifle and regarded it as an old friend. It had originally belonged to his father, who now preferred his 1873 model. He had allowed his son to start shooting with the old weapon when he was just eleven years of age, gifting it to him outright the following year.

From the first time he sighted down the Yellow Boy's octagonal barrel, Jack Parker knew that this was something at which he would excel. He couldn't have said how he knew it, but there it was. His father was vastly impressed with the boy's skill, and used to boast to his friends about the fact that a child of such tender years had such an astonishing proficiency with firearms. This was in fact something of an exaggeration, because in spite of his father's repeated efforts to show him how it was done, Jack never was able to handle a pistol and be sure of hitting the proverbial barn door. With a rifle in his hand though, nothing which ran or crawled on the earth or flew in the sky was safe. The previous summer, Jack had beaten all comers at the shooting competition and walked off with the cup at the county fair; which showed that he was not only the best shot in Mayfield, but quite possibly the whole of Benton County.

The only problem with his father's scheme for him to carry the Winchester with him all day was that it had no sling, and Jack would consequently be obliged to carry it through the streets tucked under his arm, as though he were out hunting. This was all right for the short distance from his home to the fields on the edge of town, but it would surely feel strange to march down Main Street with his rifle at the ready! Still, if that was what his father felt to be prudent, then so be it.

Jack left town and walked to a little wood which lay on the property of a farmer with whom he was on good terms. He had in the past obliged this man by shooting crows on his land, ridding the farm of many birds that would otherwise have caused a serious nuisance, with their predilection for crops and seeds. He guessed that Mr Timpson would have no objection to losing a few more of the pests. In the space of a half hour, Jack took down eleven crows and did not waste a single bullet.

The sheriff came home at the relatively godly hour of eight that night, and Jack had made some attempt at a meal for them both. It was only slices of buttered bread, along with the remains of a cut of meat they'd had two days previously, but his father was pleased at the boy's thoughtfulness. He felt that they were drawing closer each day, and thanked the Lord for it. After they had eaten and washed up the wares, Tom Parker said, 'Your birthday is coming along next week. Lordy, you'll be sixteen. It don't seem five minutes since you was a babe in arms. How the time does fly. What I wanted to say was that I'm not sure how much time I'm likely to have for shopping and so on. Is there anything you'd especially like?'

'Yes sir, I know just what I'd like. It won't cost you a cent.'

His father smiled at that and said, 'Well that

makes pleasant listening. What is it you want?'

'I want you to swear me in as a deputy, so I can help you officially.'

For a few seconds, Sheriff Parker was so taken aback that he couldn't speak. At last, he said, 'You know how to open your mouth wide boy, I'll give you that. What's brought this on?'

'I want to help you take down Timothy Carter and be revenged for Aggie Roberts.'

Tom Parker looked at his son uneasily. For the first time he wondered if this scheme of his, of getting closer to his boy by involving him in his father's work, might not be going awry. It sat ill with the sheriff to hear a boy of fifteen talk in this way of being 'revenged'. He tried not to let any of this show in his face, temporizing instead by remarking casually, 'It may not come to that. For aught we know, those boys ain't headed this way nohow. They might yet fetch up in Johnson County instead. Lord knows they got similar troubles there.'

'But if'n they do come here, you'll swear me in? I can be a part of it?'

The sheriff didn't take to being buffaloed in this way, not even by his own flesh and blood. He said as much to Jack, who shrugged and said, 'You asked what I wanted for my birthday, and I told you. I didn't think you meant it.'

For a moment, matters balanced on the edge of a knife. It looked as though the two of them might presently be at each other's throats again, just like they had been for much of the last two years or so. Sheriff Parker couldn't have borne that, not after the warmth which had grown between them over the course of the last week. He gave in, saying with the utmost reluctance, 'I'll tell you what I'll do, but I won't bargain further on this. If I get word from Cheyenne, always supposing that these fellows from Texas get that far, that they're coming to Benton County, then I'll make you a deputy pro temp.'

'What's "pro temp" mean?' asked Jack suspiciously, smelling some species of double-dealing.

'If'n you'd paid more heed during your Latin classes, you'd know,' said his father tartly, 'It's a legal term, meaning "for the time being". By which I mean I'm prepared, on the day you turn sixteen, to swear you in as a deputy, until the special circumstances are over; which is to say that any intruders have been dealt with, turfed out of the area or what have you. There, does that satisfy?'

It evidently did, for the boy's face split into a broad grin and he said warmly, 'It surely does. Thanks, Pa.'

'Maybe we can eat now and talk of something else?'

The *Cheyenne Examiner*, which was the most important newspaper in the newly formed state of Wyoming, was connected by telegraphic wire to various parts of the nation. It often carried reports that were verbatim copies of articles which had appeared in other papers across the length and breadth of the United States; always provided, of course, that these pieces had some particular relevance for the inhabitants of Wyoming. So it was that on 10 July 1891 the Examiner carried a piece which had originally been published in Texas:

No little consternation has been occasioned by recent events in the town of Paris, where the recruiting has been taking place of what is, to all intents and purposes, an army of some of the roughest types to be found in the state of Texas. Excellent remuneration is being offered to bushwhackers, road agents, those lately returned from fighting various obscure wars in Latin America and an assortment of mankillers. Those doing their best to gather together this armed body of men are believed to be agents of the WYOMING STOCK GROWERS ASSOCIATION, acting under instructions from its chief, MR TIMOTHY CARTER. We understand that he is working 'hand in glove' with a former resident of this state, MR DAVID BOOKER. Readers of this newspaper will doubtless recollect that the last time MR BOOKER was in Texas, he had to cut short his stay with the most startling abruptness. It was rumoured that he left a few steps ahead of a group of vigilant citizens, desirous of inviting MR BOOKER to a 'necktie party', following the shooting to death of a local resident who challenged MR BOOKER about his amazing luck at card play.

Your correspondent understands that the princely sum of $5 per diem is being promised to these 'soldiers of fortune' and that each has additionally been insured for $3,000. Should they be killed in action, this money will be paid to their families. It is understood that the 'regulators', as they are being described, or 'vigilantes', as others are calling them, are being furnished with a list of names of men in WYOMING who are popularly deemed to be rustlers. The aim is, allegedly, either to run these supposed miscreants out of the state or, failing that, to dispose of them humanely.

A curious circumstance, which we cannot forebear to mention, is that the acting governor of WYOMING, that well-known local character, DR AMOS BARBER, is generally admitted to be 'in' on the scheme, having provided a certain amount of money to enable the hiring of a special railroad train, which will transport the motley crew from Texas to Cheyenne; the state capital. DR BARBER, it need not be mentioned, is himself a member in good standing of the WYOMING STOCK GROWERS ASSOCIATION, the people organizing the expedition, raid, invasion or call it what you will.

Sheriff Parker received a copy of the *Cheyenne Examiner* two days after the piece was published, and it need hardly be said that reading it did little to allay his anxiety. It appeared all but a racing certainty that an army of rootless killers and ne'er-do-wells would soon be entering Wyoming, the only point of doubt being whether or not they would be coming to Mayfield and the surrounding district. Personally, he felt there was no doubt at all, because if Timothy Carter was at the back of it all, surely he would be wanting these fellows to come to his own neck of the woods and work their tricks there?

It was just as he finished reading the article from the *Cheyenne Examiner* that the street door to his office opened and in strolled Jerry Reece, the second of Sheriff Parker's deputies. Jerry had a nose for trouble and had, in some mysterious fashion, divined that he was needed back in Mayfield. The sheriff was mightily pleased to see the young man. He said gruffly, 'Thought you wasn't due back for another sennight or more? Couldn't keep away, hey?'

'Word spreads. There's a storm brewing, by all accounts. Figured that I'd be more use here than back home, soothing my mother in her grief.'

It was no secret that Jerry Reece had hated his father and had shed not a tear at his passing. He had really only gone back home for a while to comfort his mother, following her husband's death.

74

Tom Parker tried to say a few stumbling words about hoping that his deputy was bearing up under his own sorrow, but Jerry gave him such a quizzical and amused look that he soon stopped. He said, 'I dare say you've heard all that's needful. You may want to skim this piece.' He pushed the newspaper across the desk, but Jerry waved it away, saying, 'I already read that bit in the *Examiner*. Question is, what's to do next?'

'I thought that the four of us might ride out to Carter's ranch and kind of tip him the wink and warn him off whatever it is he has in mind.'

'Four? You've engaged another deputy? Or is your boy just going to tag along with us for fun?'

Mayfield was not a large town and it was all but impossible to keep anything secret there for long. It was not to be wondered at that Jerry had already heard about Jack helping round the place. The sheriff said, 'You got any objection to riding alongside my boy?'

'Not in the least. Surprised a little, I guess. I didn't think that you and he was exactly hitting it off lately.'

'Yes, things have changed somewhat. That doesn't matter. You surely didn't come haring back here to discuss my family affairs. You game for going off to see Carter this afternoon?'

'Why not?'

Jack was over at the livery stable, checking that the horses had been seen by the farrier. It had not escaped notice that the youngster had now taken to carrying his rifle wherever he went in town. His friend Pete remarked upon this, when Jack showed up that morning to check on the horses. He said, 'You going hunting or something?'

Jack reddened, unsure if he was being mocked. He said, 'My pa wants me to keep this by my side.'

'Why?'

Unwilling to talk about what he regarded as confidential business, the boy shrugged and said, 'I don't rightly know.'

Pete looked at his friend wistfully and said, 'You're changing, you know that? You never used to be so buttoned up and secretive. A fellow don't know what to make of it. It ain't just me as has noticed, neither. A heap o' folks have said things.'

'I'm not troubling anybody,' said Jack defensively, 'Just tending to my own business.'

There was a strained silence and after he had looked over the mounts, Jack saw no need to linger as he sometimes did and chat with Pete. He was sure that there would be more important things to do back at his father's office.

Jerry Reece and Jack had always got on well together. The gap in age between them was not overly substantial, Jerry being but twenty-two years of age. He was never the less a little staggered to return to town and find that Jack was now next door to being a deputy himself. When the boy walked in, Jerry greeted him warmly, saying, 'New member of the team, huh?'

'I'm just lending a hand with some chores. My pa asked me to.'

Jerry saw the rifle and thought that things might be a mite more serious than he had thought. He said, 'Somebody shoot at you, Jack?'

Jack looked over to his father, asking with his eyes how much he ought to reveal. Tom Parker said, 'Tell him the whole story, son. We've no secrets here.'

After hearing chapter and verse about what had been happening while he was away, Jerry said, 'Strikes me that the sooner we speak a few soft words to Carter, the better. Where's Brandon?'

'He'll be back about midday,' said his boss, 'When he returns, I reckon we should eat and then ride straight over to the Carter ranch and lay down the law in no small measure. Otherwise, there's going to be some blood-letting, of that I'm sure.'

Once Brandon Ross came back from his patrol, the four of them went down the road to an eating house and filled their bellies with a generous helping of pork and beans. Having done so, they went back to the office, where the two deputies collected a carbine apiece. Then they walked down Main Street towards the livery stable. People on the sidewalk stopped to stare, because the group presented a grim and forbidding spectacle, had they but known it. The sheriff was the only one of them armed only with a pistol. The sight of three men, all toting rifles under their arms was a striking one and the expression on their faces told everybody that this was no party of men going hunting. The three youngsters were amiable lads who always had a smile and a word for those they passed, in the usual way of things. Today though, they had set looks, which did not encourage anybody to call out a cheerful greeting or to wave or anything. It was as plain as a pikestaff that there was trouble in the wind.

CHAPTER 5

There was a sober air among the four of them as they rode out to Timothy Carter's spread. All felt that nervous tension that men experience when they believe they might shortly be involved in a violent confrontation. Jack was most sensitive to this atmosphere; he had butterflies in his stomach and a queasy sensation, which he recognized as the prelude to throwing up. He bit back on this feeling, for he knew that he would never again be able to look either of the two deputies in the face if he vomited in front of them at this stage of the proceedings. They would, for certain-sure, interpret this as a sign of fear. So when he felt his eyes watering and he burped slightly, bringing some bile up into his mouth, Jack focused on making his mind blank and his breathing regular. By and by, he stopped feeling sick and by the time they reached Carter's place he was in full possession of himself again.

While they had been on the road, Brandon Ross, Jerry Reece and Jack had stuck their rifles in scabbards at the front of their saddles. Once they passed the sign which informed them that they were now entering the property of Timothy Carter however, Brandon and Jerry by unspoken agreement, withdrew their rifles and carried them in their right hands, while holding the reins with their left. What it was which had prompted them to make this move, they would have been quite unable to say, but the two men both had an extra sense where danger was concerned. Uneasily, like somebody trying to play a game of whose rules he was unaware, Jack Parker too pulled his rifle out of the leather scabbard and also held it in readiness.

Usually, the yard around Carter's house was bustling with activity, but today it was deserted. Once they had halted, the sheriff and his three companions sat for a while, just watching and listening. There was no noise, either, and that was very odd. None of the usual, cheerful hubbub that you hear in a working farm or ranch. There was simply nobody around. Sheriff Parker said, 'Something's afoot, I'll tell you that for nothing.' He dismounted and gestured for the others to do likewise.

The four of them, three holding their rifles at the ready and looking round cautiously, waited for somebody to come and greet them. Some distance from the main house were the bunkhouses for the hands, but there was no sign of life around them either, from what they could see. Jack, who had keyed himself up for some kind of trouble or disturbance, found the continued silence eerie. He could feel his heart thudding within his chest and in his mouth was a faint, coppery tang, as though he had been sucking coins. He was not yet familiar with this sensation; it was the taste of raw fear.

After a few more seconds, as the tension rose inexorably and nobody spoke, they became aware of the sound of horses in the distance. It sounded like a fair number and from the steadily increasing sound, they were coming towards them. Sheriff Parker said, 'Don't none of you say or do anything. Let me do the talking. You hear me?' The other three all nodded and grunted their assent. It began to dawn on them all that what they had expected to be a routine visit to deliver a quiet warning to the rancher might be turning into a horse of another colour. They were standing there in the open and if shooting began, they would be horribly exposed to danger.

Brandon Ross said, 'Boss, don't you think we ought to get under cover and make ready for any action?'

'No,' said Sheriff Parker, 'Not if you mean ducking behind walls or hiding in barns, we're not.'

Jack felt a tightness in his throat and hoped that he wouldn't be called upon to speak for a while. He had a horrible feeling that if he tried to say anything right now, his voice would come out as either a

81

strangled croak or an undignified squeaking. Why he had wanted to try and bluff his father into appointing him deputy, he had no idea right now, and wished that he was back at the livery stable playing pitch and toss with Pete Hedstrom. He sensed that the two deputies were also twitchy and perhaps feeling a little nervous. Only his father was as calm and collected as he always was, standing there as relaxed as though he were admiring some goods in the window of a store on Main Street.

The riders came into sight up the drive that led from the road to Carter's ranch. There were five of them, and Jack had the distinct impression that they were not the usual hands one saw about town. These men had a more assured and confident air, and were dressed differently as well, a little too smartly to be wrestling with steers. One at least he knew by sight: Dave Booker, the Texan his father had spoken with on their last visit here was in the lead as the riders thundered into the yard and then reined in, close enough to the men on foot for it to seem as though they were crowding them, or at any rate attempting to do so.

Booker, who was apparently in charge, said, 'What are you men doing here? You know this is private property?'

'Don't you fool around with me now, Booker,' said Tom Parker, 'I want to speak to your boss. Is he here?

'I'm tending to his business, didn't he tell you?

82

Anything you got to say, you can deal with me.'

Sheriff Parker cast his eyes over the other riders, whose apparel was most decidedly not of the kind that was commonly seen on farm workers and ranch hands. He addressed one of the men, saying, 'Where are you from, friend? You're not from here-abouts, I'm guessing.' Instead of answering, the fellow looked at Booker, who shook his head slightly, as though to indicate that he should say nothing. This irked the sheriff and prompted him to say softly, 'You know, Booker, that obstructing a peace officer in the execution of his duties is likely to lead you into all sorts of difficulties. Were I you, I wouldn't even think of trying it.'

'Yes, but you see, you ain't me. You want Mr Carter, he's gone off for a day or two and I'm running the place now. You don't have a warrant or nothing, you'd best be getting along. Take your snot-nosed kid with you. That the best you can do in the way o' deputies round here?'

Never in all his life had Jack heard anybody speak in such a way to his father. He trembled, wondering what would next chance. He could not imagine that anybody would be able to treat Mayfield's sheriff with such frank contempt, at least not without a reckoning coming to them.

If Sheriff Parker was in the slightest degree put out or offended by being spoken to like this, he gave no external sign. The expression on his face remained unaltered and his tone of voice, when he

83

replied to Booker, was as calm and level as usual. He said, 'I suppose that Carter's gone off to Cheyenne, has he?'

Dave Booker looked momentarily surprised, before replying, 'I didn't say so.'

The sheriff suddenly grinned and said, 'You just told me. Thanks for confirming what I suspicioned.'

Booker scowled and then thrust a hand inside his jacket. Jerry Reece at once brought up his rifle, worked a cartridge into the breech, and drew down on the Texan, thinking that the man was going for a hidden weapon. This action on Jerry's part caused one of the men riding with Booker to jerk his pistol out, which in turn made Brendon Ross think that it would be the smart dodge to raise his own weapon and cock it. As for Jack, he hardly knew what to do with his own gun. His father said urgently, 'No, no, that's not what I want at all. All of you, put up your weapons. There's no need for shooting.'

For a tense few seconds, his deputies kept their rifles trained on Booker and his men. Two of those men had pistols in their hands and nobody seemed quite sure about what was going to happen next. Then Dave Booker chuckled and withdrew his hand from within his jacket. In it was grasped a silver cigar case, from which he extracted one of the aniseed-flavoured cheroots that he was so fond of. He lit it and remarked to nobody in particular, 'Well, that looked like it might have got a little lively!'

In obedience to their boss's command, the two deputies lowered their rifles. Booker's men then holstered their pistols. Sheriff Parker walked up to Booker's horse and said very quietly, 'Here's a message for Mr Carter. You and these boys best take heed as well. I'll have no more killings in this area. Nor will I have any gangs of bandits racing around the county. You carry on down this present road, Booker, and you and your boss are going to call the lightning down on your heads. Don't do it. Just back off now, while there's still time enough.'

'You sound like a man who's afeared,' said Booker, 'One who ain't got the stomach for trouble.'

'I give you the warning. You don't heed it, that's your affair.' The sheriff turned to his deputies and son, saying, 'Come on, you fellows. Our business here is done.' They mounted up and rode off, while Dave Booker and his companions watched them impassively. Once they were clear of Carter's place, Tom Parker moved alongside his son and said, 'You all right, Jack?'

'I guess so. I thought there was going to be fighting. Shooting and such.'

'The idea scare you?'

For a moment, it was on the tip of Jack's tongue to deny this suggestion and to claim that he'd been ready for anything back there, but he couldn't bring himself to tell the lie. He said instead, 'I was frightened, sir. I don't mind owning to it.'

85

To his surprise, Jack's father replied, 'Good. That's just how it should be.'

In response to his son's interrogative glance, Sheriff Parker said, 'I could never trust a man who says that he ain't scared when a gunfight is looming. Either he's a liar or he's a madman. I wouldn't care to have either by my side when the chips are down.'

'I thought you might think I was soft.'

'You, son? Not for a moment.'

'What happens now?'

'What did you fellows make of all that?' asked the sheriff, raising his voice a little, so that they knew that he was not just engaged in some private conversation, 'Anybody have any thoughts on what should be the next move?'

'You think it's certain now that this train-load of Texans is heading here?' asked Brandon Ross, 'You think that Carter's gone to Cheyenne to meet them?'

'Oh, yes,' said the sheriff, 'I've always been of that opinion. It's the only thing that fits all that we know of this business. They'll have a list of names, and once they come, they'll ride round, killing and burning, until all those who've settled in here in recent years move off their land. Carter'll tear up the fences and return all the fields to open range.'

Once they got back to Mayfield, Tom Parker said to his son, 'I got a little job for you, if you think you're up to it.'

'What is it, sir?'

86

'Your friends from school all know what's what, don't they? About what happens at home, what their folk talk of at table and so on?'

'I reckon, yes.'

'Suppose you spend the rest of this day just talking to your friends and trying to gauge what the mood is? I know what men say to my face, but I've no notion at all what they say in their own homes.'

'It sounds like spying,' said Jack uneasily, 'I don't know that I like the sound of it.'

His father did not speak for a minute and then said slowly, 'I don't know that I care for it either, boy. If I was asking you just for the sake of gossip and being curious, your objection would be a sound one – but I'm not. This is life and death. What's a little subterfuge, compared with saving lives?'

A philosopher might well have been inclined to debate this point with the sheriff of Mayfield, but Jack Parker was no logician, and neither was he much of a one for metaphysics. He did as his father had bid him, and went off to find out what he could about the views and opinion of the town's citizens, as regarding the idea of armed invaders in and around Mayfield.

Starting with Pete Hedstrom at the livery stable, Jack wandered around town that afternoon, catching up with his former schoolmates and listening to their views. More often than not, they framed their statements with direct reference to what they had heard from their parents, typically, beginning by saying, 'My pa says. . . .' or 'It's like Ma told me the other day. . . .' Almost without exception, their parents appeared to favour the homesteaders over Timothy Carter and the other long-established ranchers. Talking this over with his father that evening, Jack could not see why this was.

'See, son,' his father said, after Jack had reported back on what he had managed to pick up about the mood of the town, 'Those hands from the ranches spend money, but more often than not in the saloon. They cause a heap o' trouble too, into the bargain. Getting drunk, insulting folk, bothering young women and suchlike. The homesteaders are families for the most part. They want to build something up. They might not be spending a whole lot, but they're decent folk and they go towards making this a good town to live in. Times are changing, the old ways are gone. Folk here want to live the way people do in big cities, back east. They want trams and telephones, not drunken cowboys brawling in the streets.'

'Will they join you then, I mean if it comes to fighting?'

Tom Parker rubbed his chin and said meditatively, 'That, as you might say, is the big question. They'd rather not. They want me to deal with all this by my own self. But I think if there's a bunch of no-goods from outside fetching up here and causing bloodshed, then they might. They just might.'

According to the best information available to Sheriff Parker, which he shared with his son, the train containing the fifty or more 'regulators' recruited in Texas was due to arrive in Cheyenne on the Tuesday. The wires between Texas and Wyoming had been fairly humming, and the sheriff knew all that he needed to for his purposes. A contact just across the state line in Colorado informed him that somebody had bought thirty horses and was arranging for them to be transported to Cheyenne, arriving at about the same time as the train from Texas. This tied in with word from Paris, that only about twenty horses were being carried in an extra car on the train. Presumably it was thought that acquiring mounts in Colorado would not be noticed as much as buying them in Wyoming would. The aim was, Sheriff Parker supposed, to assemble this body of armed men, ride into Benton County, kill a bunch of people and then leave the area as swiftly as could be, before there was time to organize any kind of opposition. He would have to move pretty sharpish himself, if he were to have any hope of averting what promised to be a large-scale shedding of blood.

The day after he nearly clashed with Carter's Texan range detective, Sheriff Parker found himself up against the man again. This is what happened. It may well have been true, as the sheriff contended, that the vast majority of the newcomers to Wyoming were as honest as anybody else, but inevitably, bad apples were to be found among them, as in any other large body of men and women. In short, there were real stock thieves scattered here and there, and such men were not wholly a figment of Timothy Carter's imagination.

Jack was, at his father's instruction, polishing various bits and pieces in the office and trying to make it look a little smarter and better kept. Now that both deputies were back, his duties had become a little more menial and Jack wondered if this would change if his father really did agree to swear him in as a deputy on his birthday, which fell in a few days.

It was the morning after the little run-in with Dave Booker and his friends, and from what Jack could make out, his father had wired Cheyenne to see if he could pick up any information on what was happening with the train from Texas. Apart from waiting for an answer to his enquiry, nothing else much was happening. Brandon Ross was writing up some report and Sheriff Parker was reading through notices that he had received, chiefly relating to men wanted for various offences. It seemed to Jack that he was the only one of the three actually doing anything which was at all like work that day. As he polished the brass knob of the street door, somebody attempted to open it from without. He stepped back to allow this person to enter the office.

The clerk from the hardware store down the street had never before had cause to venture into the sheriff's office and he looked about him uncertainly. Tom Parker said, 'Mr Jackson, what might I be doing for you this morning?'

Jackson, a fussy and old maidish man of fifty, said, 'I'm not in general one to mix myself up with things as don't concern me, but somebody come in the store not five minutes since and told me something you ought to know.'

'What's that, Mr Jackson?' asked the sheriff, 'You can speak freely here, you know.'

'Fellow said he'd passed along the way and seen what looked to him like a party of lawmen. They had two men with them, hands tied like prisoners. The whole lot of 'em were heading for Mr Carter's ranch.'

No sooner had the little man got these words out than Sheriff Parker was on his feet and going over to the rack of firearms at the back of the office. He selected a scattergun and as he did so said sharply to his son and Brandon Ross, 'Bestir yourselves, the pair of you. We need to move like lightning. Mr Jackson, I'm obliged to you for the information, sir.'

The storekeeper left, seemingly alarmed at the sudden flurry of activity. 'Scribble a note for Jerry,' said the sheriff, to nobody in particular, 'Tell him we've gone up to the Carter place.' Jack did this hurriedly, before snatching up his rifle and racing out the door after his father and the deputy. The

91

three of them fairly ran down Main Street to the livery stable and then waited impatiently while Pete Hedstrom tacked up three horses. The second this was done, Sheriff Parker vaulted into the saddle and urging the other two on, set off up the road at a canter, causing passers-by to remark uneasily that their sheriff seemed in the deuce of a hurry and that maybe something was up.

As they speeded up to a gallop along the road leading north out of town, Jack was gripped by a terrible fear that they would soon be coming across another hanging body. He had seen more than enough of such things in the space of a few weeks to last him a lifetime, and he prayed that it would not be so, that they would be in time to save the lives of the men who had evidently been taken up to Timothy Carter's ranch.

Had Dave Booker and his Texan friends been content to take off the two rustlers and hang them in some out of the way place, then Sheriff Parker and his two assistants would most certainly have had no chance at all of preventing their being lynched. Booker, though, was a cruel man, with the sort of playful streak that you see in small boys who torment kittens or pull the wings off flies. He had a mind to see the men he had captured suffer some mental agonies before they kicked out their lives on the end of a rope. Something put it into his mind to stage a mock trial before disposing of the two men. The verdict and sentence would never be in doubt to Booker and his boys, but the victims themselves might be given a false hope, which would make their ultimate fate all the more bitter.

When the sheriff, flanked by his deputy and son, rode into the yard in front of Carter's imposing house, it was to find two men sitting on horseback with their hands bound and men holding the bridles of the horses, to forestall any desperate attempt to gallop away and escape. Booker, who was also seated on horseback was facing the men and behind him were a half dozen other riders. The scene put Jack Parker in mind of children playing at courtrooms, with Booker as the judge and the men behind him adopting the part of a jury. His face, when he turned round and saw who the visitors were, was anything but welcoming.

'Care to tell me what's going on here?' enquired Sheriff Parker affably. 'I didn't know any better and I might mistake this for a necktie party. I hope I'm wrong, mind.'

'This is no business of yours,' said Booker, 'Whyn't you just go back to town and leave us to this?'

'Can't be done,' said the sheriff, still in a pleasant tone of voice, as though he genuinely regretted having to disrupt another man's enjoyment, 'Those men, who I understand have been taken in the act of theft, are arrested by me. They're my prisoners. Sorry about that.'

Booker smiled and said, 'They worth risking your life for?'

Brandon Ross was sure that his boss was about to back down, facing as they did odds of three to one against men who would probably not hesitate to shoot them down if it came to the point. But Jack recognized that tone in his father's voice, and knew full well that somebody was in for a dreadful shock presently.

Booker should have known better than to lower his guard, just because a man was speaking pleasantly and smiling apologetically. He was revelling in the sense of power which came from having a lawman speak so to him, and didn't think it significant that this same sheriff was walking his horse forward while chatting to Booker like he might have been a long-lost brother. It was not until Tom Parker produced from nowhere a sawn-off scatter gun, cocking both barrels with audible clicks as he did so and aiming it straight into Dave Booker's face, that the other man realized the peril he was in.

The thing had happened so swiftly that neither Booker nor his companions had yet had a chance to respond, when the sheriff said quietly in a completely different voice, 'You all should know that I've taken first pull on the trigger here. I so much as sneeze or fart and I'm like to blow your head clean off your shoulders, Booker. You counsel your men to stay still and not go for their weapons.'

'Do like he says.'

'Hell, he's bluffing,' said one member of the impromptu jury, 'he ain't a-goin' to shoot.'

94

'No,' said Booker in a lazy and unhurried way, 'He's not bluffing. Just you boys do as he says.'

'I'm going to come up close to you and take that gun from your holster,' said Sheriff Parker, looking straight into Booker's eyes. 'Don't think of resisting, for it'll be the death of you. Maybe I'll get killed in what happens next, but you'll still be dead, whatever next chances.' Having delivered himself of these words, he walked his horse forward very slowly, never once taking his eyes off Booker. Then, making sure to keep the shotgun pointing straight at the other, he reached across and plucked the pistol from Booker's belt. 'There now,' he said, 'That went well enough, didn't it?'

Aware as he was that Booker was a cold-hearted killer, Jack could not help but admire the man for his coolness under what must have been a very nerve-racking and trying experience. He wondered if he himself would be able to remain so calm and collected with a scattergun aimed right at his face in that way. From the way that Booker was taking it, he and Jack's father might as well have been having a beer together. 'Brandon, you make those two prisoners ready to travel. Don't take your eyes from them and be ready to shoot them too, if they show any signs of wanting to escape. Take them over to the entrance to the yard. You too, Jack. I'll follow on with Mr Booker here.'

Taking no notice of the other men in the yard, Tom Parker said to Booker, 'Here's how we'll play it.

You're coming back to town with me. Any sign of treachery, something in the way of an ambush by your friends say, and I promise you that you'll be the first to die. Even if somebody shoots me from cover, I'm bound to twitch my finger as I die and despatch you in the process. That clear?'

'That's clear,' said Booker, he raised his voice a little and addressed his men, telling them, 'You fellows set where you are. Don't follow on. I'll be back soon enough.'

Once the little procession was clear of Timothy Carter's land and on the road to Mayfield, one of the rescued men said fulsomely, 'Sheriff, you got no idea how grateful me and my partner are. I truly thought that I was about to die.'

'Yes, we're mighty thankful. Maybe you could tell your men to free our hands now. It ain't easy to ride like this.'

'You men live round these parts?' asked Tom Parker casually, 'I don't recollect your faces.'

'No, we're from over in Johnson County.'

'What are you doing here?'

There was an awkward silence, which was broken only by Booker chuckling out loud. He said, 'Ask 'em how we came across them, why don't you?'

The sheriff ignored Dave Booker and said, 'Well? Cat got your tongues?' to the two men. They said nothing.

Sheriff Parker had so arranged things that Booker was riding at the head of the party, so that he could cover the man from behind with his scattergun. The two men whom he had snatched, as it were, from the jaws of death, rode a little behind him, with Brandon Ross and Jack Parker bringing up the rear. They rode on in silence for a while, until Booker said, 'You really going to take me all the way to town?'

'That I am,' said Sheriff Parker, 'Why do you ask?'

''Cause I'm wondering if you're fixing for to make me ride down Main Street like a prisoner, when all I done was catch some stock thieves, men as the real law never touches.'

'I'll tell you how it is, Booker,' said the sheriff. 'I don't want men in the town to think that Carter and his boys are running Benton County, nor nothing like it. Seeing his chief man been led around at the point of a gun, I'd say that was mighty wholesome for them to observe. What they call an "object lesson", I believe.'

'You know I'm like to kill you, you do any such thing?'

'We'll see what we see.'

In the event, Sheriff Parker did indeed lead Booker and his two prisoners down Main Street, which caused no small amount of interest among those walking along the sidewalk that day. When they got to the office, the sheriff dismounted and encouraged Booker to do likewise. Then he said, 'I understand that you wish to lay an information against these men for stealing or attempting to steal

97

some livestock. Have I got that right?' When Booker simply shrugged, too furious to speak, the sheriff carried on, saying, 'Unless those steers were your property, then I can't take a statement from you. The owner will have to attend here. I'm guessing that'd be Timothy Carter?'

'He's in Cheyenne.'

'Well, when he gets back, be sure to tell him to attend my office.'

Booker was clearly irritated by this exchange, and when it was over, said, 'How about handing me back my pistol?'

'Mood you're in?' said Sheriff Parker, with a laugh. 'You're like to shoot me down on the spot! Get somebody to call for it tomorrow, when you've cooled down a bit.'

After Booker had left, muttering curses, imprecations and threats of bloody revenge under his breath, one of the two men who had lately escaped summary hanging said, 'Sheriff, you were magnificent. We can't thank you enough.'

Tom Parker turned and eyed the two men coldly. He said, 'I got no more love for rustlers than the next man. You two can spend the night in my cell and then if the owner of the steers doesn't show up, I'll release you on a bail bond. But I tell you now, I reckon you'd be well advised to leave Benton County while you've the use of your limbs. I'm not likely to rescue you a second time.'

After Brandon Ross had locked the two men in

the cramped little cell at the rear of the sheriff's office and Jack had taken the horses to the livery stable, the sheriff and his son spoke seriously. Or rather Sheriff Parker spoke and his son listened. 'You still want to try your hand at being a deputy? You've not repented of the notion, after seeing what you have in the last few days?'

'No sir, I reckon not.'

The older man sighed and said, 'I pledged my word and I won't break it, least of all to my own kin. Three days from now, on your birthday, you still want that I should do it, I'll swear you in. At least 'til this business is settled. But I beg you to think the better of it.'

CHAPTER 6

Timothy Carter did not show up to make a statement about the theft of his cattle, and so the day after he had rescued them from being lynched, Sheriff Parker freed the two rustlers; repeating his earnest advice that they should leave Benton County as swiftly and quietly as they were able. After their narrow escape, he formed the impression that they were minded to heed his warnings. After ridding himself of his unwanted guests, the sheriff read a wire which had just been delivered to the office. It informed him that the train from Paris, with the 'regulators' aboard, had now left Paris and would be likely to arrive in Cheyenne that very night. Allowing for a day or so to get themselves organized and prepared, that might mean that the Texans would be hitting Benton County, if that were indeed their aim, on the day after tomorrow: Jack's birthday.

Jack watched his father covertly, while tidying up

the range and black-leading those parts that looked shabby. It was clear that the wire which had just been handed to him was enough to cause his father some perturbation. He guessed, quite correctly, that it had some reference to the men heading into Wyoming from Texas. Tom Parker glanced up and, seeing his son's eyes upon him, said, 'I just received word that this damned train is on the move and heading in this direction. There's a chance that this'll not concern us, but I wouldn't lay odds on it. Day after tomorrow is when your birthday falls, isn't it?'

'It is, yes sir.'

'All I'll say is this. If those boys are leaving Cheyenne and look like to come here, then morning of your birthday, I'll swear you in. Only 'til this affair is done with, mind. After that, we'll talk about your future.'

'Thanks, Pa.'

'Don't thank me, you young fool. You little know what you're asking for,' replied his father gruffly, 'Why you can't be content with studying in books is more than I can say. Still, there it is. You're full young and want to see some excitement.'

Sheriff Parker was being less than candid with his son. He had no intention of placing his only child in hazard, and for all that he was ready to have the boy appointed, in theory at least, a deputy, he was not about to see Jack ride against a band of hardened wretches such as these Texans appeared to be.

101

He would find a way of keeping the boy safe, even if it meant locking him up.

Later that morning, Jerry Reece came in and announced that there was great enthusiasm among the homesteaders for joining a legally constituted posse and facing down Carter and his bully boys. It was a question, now, of which way the town would jump when the knife reached the bone. 'Time's come, I guess' said the sheriff, 'to ask folk here which side they're going to be on. There's no room left for shilly-shallying, and the men will either have to be for law and order, or on the side of a crew of Texan freebooters.'

'That how you'll present the case to 'em?' asked Reece.

'I reckon,' was the laconic response. 'Time's come to lay down,' said Sheriff Parker abruptly, 'Let's see who's got what cards and who'll be with us, now that the time is here.' He stood up and said to Jerry and Jack, 'You boys come with me.'

'Where are we going, sir?' asked Jack.

'In the first instance, we'll pay a little visit to that mayor of ours and see if he's grown a backbone yet.'

It might have been his imagination, but Jack fancied there was an air of tension on the streets of Mayfield, the feeling one gets sometimes when a thunderstorm is about to arrive. His skin prickled, and as he walked alongside his father to Mayor Collins' home, Jack thought that the eyes of all those they passed were trained upon them expectantly.

Perhaps it was as his father suggested, that the time was drawing near when the men living in the town would be forced to make a choice and declare themselves to be on one side or the other. Nobody likes being put into such a position, and the man who buffalos others into making a stand is seldom likely to win any popularity contests.

The mayor had evidently been anticipating a visit from the sheriff, because the three of them were hardly through the door, before he began expostulating angrily about being placed in a false position. 'What it is, Parker, is where you've been trying to persuade me to sanction some kind of battle against some of the most important individuals hereabouts. Well, it won't answer and there's an end to the matter!'

Sheriff Parker did not get agitated, merely saying quietly, 'There's better than fifty armed men, mercenary wretches, from all that I'm able to apprehend, heading this way to commit murder. You're telling me that's no concern of mine?'

'Don't try and bluster with me,' said the mayor, his voice rising an octave and increasing in pitch, 'Mr Carter's wired me about that. There's nothing untoward, these men are regulators. They'll patrol the range and look out for rustlers. Any they find will be handed over to you, there'll be due process.' Then, in a quieter voice – Jack thought that 'wheedling' would aptly describe Mayor Collins' new tone – he said, 'Come on Tom, you and me

103

have known each other for the longest time. Surely to goodness we ain't going to fall out over a trifling matter such as this? You wouldn't get crosswise to me for the sake of a few stock thieves, would you?'

Shaking his head sadly, Sheriff Parker said, 'I thought the better of you, Bill.' Turning to his deputy and son, he said, 'Let's go. We've business to attend to.'

As they left the room, Mayor Collins said, 'Don't you do nothing hasty now, Tom. You hear what I tell you?'

After they were out of the house, Jack asked his father what would now happen. 'I suppose that what next happens,' replied his father slowly, 'is that I go ahead and start recruiting for a posse. I'm damned if I know how I'm going to pay them, not without the mayor's goodwill and co-operation, but there it is. If we don't make a stand, then we're altogether lost. I sit by now and watch a heap of murders being done for a base motive, what kind of sheriff am I? What kind of man either, if it comes to that?'

'You going to start today?' asked Jerry Reece, 'Time's running low, from what I can see.'

'Those Texans'll be hitting Cheyenne this very night. They can hardly start moving in on us until tomorrow, or most likely the next day,' said Sheriff Parker slowly. 'I can't raise a body of men and then tell them to sit around waiting. Especially where as things stand, I'm like enough to have to pay 'em out of my own pocket. No. I'll speak to folk tomorrow evening and then ask them to stand by. Lord, I could do without this!'

Tom Parker was pretty good, as a rule, at calculating to the finest point when to strike and when to hold fire. He could hardly be blamed on this occasion for hesitating until he was certain of what was going on. The following day was quiet as could be, until about eleven in the morning, when the sheriff had it in mind to go to one or two saloons and see if any men were desirous of joining him in enforcing the law. Jack was sitting in the office, waiting to see if his father would tolerate his son accompanying him to a bar-room. Truth to tell, he didn't think it at all likely that he would be allowed to go along on the recruiting drive.

There had been no word that morning of what the train-load of gunmen might be up to, the line being down between Mayfield and the state capital. Nothing was thought of this until later, it not being an uncommon occurrence for Mayfield to be temporarily cut off from the rest of the world in this way. Just as the sheriff was locking away various papers and preparing to send his son home, so that he himself could visit a few saloons, the door to the street opened and two ragged and ill-kempt individuals entered the office. The men, grizzled oldsters, were, from the look of them, trappers or hunters. 'Evenin' captain,' said one to the sheriff, 'Thought as we ought let you know what's what, 'way over yonder.'

'What's that?'

'Heap o' shootin', some miles north of here, 'bout five hours since.'

'Perhaps the two of you would care for some coffee? Jack, could you see to it please? Sit down and make yourselves comfortable and tell what you've seen.'

The two men were, it appeared, as the sheriff had guessed, trappers. They had been passing along a ridge when they'd heard shooting, a considerable amount of it. To their ears, it sounded just like a gun battle being fought. Curious to know what was going on, they proceeded cautiously to a point where they had a good view of what was happening. A large number of men, some dozens, were besieging a log cabin. Every so often, shots would be fired from the narrow windows of this little dwelling, towards the attackers, whereupon a fusillade of shots would be directed against the wooden hut. This went on for about an hour; the men had no idea how long the siege had been in progress before they arrived on the scene.

The trappers had the impression that when they first sat down to watch the show, the firing from the cabin had been stronger and was now slackening off a little. The conclusion they drew was that at first there had been several defenders and that maybe some had been hit and put out of action. Then there was a long spell with no shooting at all, and

106

the two watching men speculated that perhaps the last of the men in the cabin had now been hit. This proved not to be the case, however, for the door was flung open and a man came charging out, with a rifle in one hand and pistol in the other. The emergence of this fellow seemed to take the men surrounding the cabin by surprise. He blazed away with his pistol as he ran, and then, when that was empty, he cast it aside and raised the rifle to his shoulder. Then the attackers recollected themselves and a dozen men fired at him, sending him sprawling to the dirt before he even had the chance to get off one shot with the rifle.

'Was that all,' said the sheriff in a low voice, 'meaning, did you boys leave at that point?'

'No, we didn't like to leave at once and draw attention to our own selves,' said one of the men, 'Being witnesses to murder, like, we thought as they might decide to do away with us as well, you see.'

'Smart move. So what did you do?'

'We waited. After they'd kicked the body about some, they went into the cabin and there was a couple o' shots. Then they saddle up and leave.'

'And you came straight here, to do your civic duty and report a felony?' asked the sheriff, in a gently ironic tone. 'That's mighty public-spirited of you, boys.'

'Me and m'partner,' said one of the men, 'Was wondering if there's any sort of reward at all. Also, we found this on the dead man. Thought it might

be important.' He delved into his clothing and produced a cheap notebook, which was smeared and
bedaubed with dried blood. 'Anyways, you might be
wantin' it.'

A glimmer of hope showed in Sheriff Parker's
eyes. He said, 'You men want paying. Happen
you're running low on cash money?' The two of
them nodded eagerly, clearly half hoping that they
would be handed a bag of gold or something of the
sort. 'What it is,' continued the sheriff, 'is that you
fellows look to me like you can handle yourselves
well, maybe you fought in the war. I'm raising a
posse to take on those men you seen do this thing.
Five dollars a day. You want in?'

But it appeared that neither of the trappers did
want in. Upon discovering that there was no reward
to be had of a monetary nature, they were keen to
shake the dust of the town from their feet and make
off back into the wilderness. After they had left, the
sheriff said to his son, 'Jack, you've a fine reading
voice. Would you care to tell what is written here?'

Jack Parker took the notebook, trying to avoid
touching the bloodstains and leafed through it.
Most was taken up with notes of various financial
transactions, but the last few pages were in the form
of a personal statement, which was signed at the
end with the name of Johnathon Cade. He looked
up and said to his father and Jerry, 'Hey, wasn't
Cade the name of that fellow as was here a few days
since? Wanting to stake claim on his land?'

108

'It's the same man,' said his father grimly, 'Read it out loud, son.'

Clearing his throat, Jack read, 'Me and Pete were getting breakfast when the attack took place. Pete started out and I told him to look out and that there was danger. He is shot but not dead yet. He is awful sick but still shooting back at those damned villains. It is now two hours since the first shot and the bullets is coming like hail. I must wait on Pete.'

Jack looked up and said, 'The writing gets a bit raggedy, like it was done in a real hurry. I think this page was written later than the first. Shall I go on?'

'Yes, read it all son.'

'Pete is dead. Them fellows is in such shape I can't get at them. They are shooting from the stable and river and back of the cabin. Well, they stopped shelling of the house now. I guess they are going to fire this place. I think I'll make a break for it. Goodbye boys, if I never see you again.'

After Jack had finished, the three of them sat in silence for a minute; perhaps as a mark of respect for the dead homesteader who had chronicled the last hours of his life. Then, Sheriff Parker broke the silence, saying briskly, 'Well, the time is upon us, I guess. I waited long enough. Jerry, you ride round the homesteaders. Spread word that if they want to fight back, now's the time. Tell 'em to gather all the men they can and come to town. I'm going to rouse this place and alert them to their danger. I never heard the like, fifty armed men from the south riding down on us in this way. It isn't to be borne!'

'What would you have me do, sir?' asked Jack.

'You come with me. You can go errands for me, I guess?'

'Does that mean I'm like a regular deputy now?'

Despite the gravity of the situation, Sheriff Parker chuckled. He said, 'Lord, you remind me of me at such an age. I suppose that you're a-wanting your birthday present today and not wait 'til tomorrow, is that the strength of it?'

Jack had the grace to look a little abashed and simply shrugged his shoulders. His father went over to his desk and rummaged around in a drawer. Jerry Reece stood uncertainly at the door; on the point of leaving and not wishing to intrude upon what looked to him like purely personal, family business. Sheriff Parker growled to him, 'Don't hover on the threshold like that. It makes me nervous. Come back a moment, for I need you to witness a document.'

Jerry walked over to the sheriff and said quietly, 'You sure about this, boss? Things are like to get pretty damned lively 'fore long. You don't want your own kin in on it, seems to me, not if it can be helped.'

'True as far as it goes, but the fact is that I need men by my side as I know won't cut and run when the going gets a little hot. This boy of mine has his faults, as God he knows, but he'll stick to me like a cocklebur. You never hear where blood is thicker than water?'

'I heared something of the sort from my grand-pappy,' admitted the deputy, 'But I still got my doubts about this.'

'Happen so, but one of us is sheriff and the other deputy. Just you stand to, while I administer this oath.'

Handing a crumpled sheet of paper to his son, Sheriff Parker said soberly, 'If you're really resolved upon this, then read out these words. Recollect, though, that this is a sworn oath. It's no light matter.'

A little awed at his father's tone of voice, Jack took the proffered sheet and spoke the following words, 'I, Jack Parker, do solemnly swear that I will perform with fidelity the duties of the office to which I have been appointed this day and which I am about to assume. I do solemnly swear to support the constitution of the United States and to faith-fully perform the duties of the office of deputy sheriff for the state of Wyoming. I further swear that I have not promised or given, nor will I give any fee, gift, gratuity or reward for this office or for aid in procuring this office, that I will not take any fee, gift or bribe or gratuity for returning any person as a juror or for making any false return of any process and that I will faithfully execute the office of deputy sheriff to the best of my knowledge and ability, agreeably to law.' Jack paused after making this dec-laration and then confessed candidly, 'I don't know what some of those words mean.'

'Means you're going to deal straight and do nothing underhand,' explained his father, 'Now I have to tell you that I have witnessed your oath on this seventeenth day of July in this year of grace, eighteen hundred and ninety one. Jerry, set your mark on this and then me and the boy, I should say, the new deputy, will also sign it.'

Once all this had been satisfactorily completed, Sheriff Parker said, 'Jerry, you cut along now and try and get those settlers moving. Me and this new deputy will pay a few visits in town. I don't aim to see any more murders committed in my jurisdiction, not while I can do anything about it.'

After Jerry Reece had departed, Jack said to his father, 'I don't need to worry about all that stuff about bribes and gratuities, do I sir?'

'All you need to worry about, son, is keeping that rifle of yours near at hand and being prepared, if necessary, to fire it at men.' He went to the desk drawer again and pulled out a little piece of metal, which he handed to Jack, saying, 'Here, you'd better wear this or folk'll say there's something irregular about the whole thing.' When Jack looked down at what lay in his hands, he saw a small, silvery, six-pointed star, with rounded points. In the middle of this star were inscribed the words, 'Deputy Sheriff'. Awestruck, he looked up at his father.

'Should I pin it on my jacket?'

'I should say that's a right good notion, son.' As

he looked at his son, so eager and boyish on the one hand and so grown up on the other, Tom Parker felt his eyes misting over unexpectedly. He turned away, furious with himself for allowing such foolish emotion to get the better of him.

Jack said, 'Is everything all right?'

'Yes,' growled his father, determined not to reveal any sign of his feelings. 'Let's get on with things, the day is wearing away.'

It was still not yet noon, and the Star of the North saloon had only two customers, farmers from out of town come to do a little trading. Sheriff Parker went to the barman, whom he knew well, and said, 'A very good morning to you, Roland. Business a little slack today?'

'Ah, it'll pick up in an hour or so. What can I do for you today, sheriff?'

'If you've no objection, you can pass the word to those who come in here that I'm looking to raise a posse. Men who will be prepared to hazard their lives standing up to a bunch of armed invaders.'

The barman stared at Sheriff Parker for a moment and then shook his head. 'As bad as that, hey? Knew it was in the wind, didn't know it would be upon us so quick.'

'It's not of my choosing. But tell me now, what's your own view of the thing, which is to say Carter and the homesteaders?'

Flattered to have his opinions solicited in this way and never averse to speaking his mind, John Roland

113

thought for a second and then said, 'You ask anybody in Mayfield that question a twelvemonth ago and I'll warrant we all would o' give you the self-same answer. Namely, Mr Timothy Carter is this town's biggest benefactor. Why, the money his cowboys throw around in the town is something to behold. But you know that, sheriff. These days though, folk are thinking more about how times have changed. The range is vanishing, day of the cowboy is over. I reckon the future lies with them settlers. They've families, they want to be prosperous and they'll bring money to the town. Maybe not this year, but it won't be long.'

Tom Parker's private view was that Roland was a long-winded son of a bitch, but he listened patiently to what the fellow had to say. When the barkeeper had finished, he asked him, 'So you think that people will oppose any of these hired guns that Carter has brought into the county?'

'Damn right they will! I heard about those southerners. We don't want them here and I'll take oath you'll have a dozen men sign up to drive them off.'

'I'll be needing a few more than a dozen.'

'Stand on me, sheriff. I'll give the word out.'

After making the rounds of other saloons and stores, as well as stopping some of the men he knew and telling them what was afoot, Sheriff Parker was moderately satisfied with the way the day went. Jack had taken little part in the proceedings, merely standing next to his father and keeping his mouth

114

shut. Had he but known it, Jack was the object of remark by a number of people who saw the two of them that day, with observations being made along the lines that the youngster was a chip off the old block and no mistake. The fact that the boy was sporting a deputy's badge surprised nobody. It was more or less assumed in Mayfield that boys would follow in their father's footsteps, farmers raising farmers, storekeepers raising storekeepers and so on. That being so, it was only natural that Sheriff Parker's son should be trained up to become a lawman himself.

It was when they called in at the telegraph office that the sheriff realized that things might be even more serious than he had hitherto supposed. Not only was the line to Cheyenne still down, but so were others leading south. The clerk in the office did not think for a moment that this could be coincidental. He shook his head and said, 'Mark what I say, there's mischief in this. Somebody wants this town cut off from the whole, entire world. Any idea why that might be, sheriff? Bank robbery planned, would you say, or something worse?'

Jack watched his father's face as he replied, and suddenly noticed just how worn and bowed down by cares Tom Parker appeared to be. He had an urgent desire to take some of the burden from his father's shoulders and transfer it to his own. So it was that before Sheriff Parker had a chance to reply to the clerk, Jack cut in and said, 'It's a sight more serious than a piddling little robbery, Mr Archer. This is an assault upon our statehood by a band of armed marauders!'

Ezekiel Archer, who had known Jack all his life, looked at the boy in amazement. He could not have been more surprised, had he heard his cat suddenly begin to express an opinion. There was an uncomfortable silence and Jack Parker wondered if he had somehow overstepped the mark and put his father out of countenance. This proved not to be the case though, for Sheriff Parker said, after a pause, 'It's just like my deputy says, Zeke. This here is more than just a few fellows on the scout, looking to knock over a bank. It's next door to being an invasion.'

After they left the telegraph office, Jack more than half expected his father to roast him for speaking out of turn, but nothing of the kind happened. Instead, Tom Parker said, 'You're changing son, you know that?'

'Is that a good thing, sir? You ain't vexed with me?'

'Not a bit of it. You're doing just fine, from all I'm able to apprehend.'

Their visits around the businesses of Mayfield served to confirm what the sheriff had suspected: that people in the town were far from happy about a bunch of southerners being shipped into the county to kill those who had chosen to settle thereabouts. The wild days, when men could ride

116

around with guns in their hands, doing pretty much as they pleased, were gone. Now, the folk in this town wished only to lead peaceable and industrious lives, getting on with their affairs without let or hindrance. In their minds, they had over the last twelve months or so weighed the matter up in their hearts and concluded that homesteaders and their families would tend more in this direction than having Mayfield surrounded once more by open range and visited periodically by drunken cowboys making whoopee, no matter how much cash money such roughnecks might spend in the saloons and stores.

There was, too, another factor in play, and this was that the older men of the town, now clerking in stores or engaged in other mundane occupations, had many of them fought almost thirty years earlier in the great war between the states. Aware though they were of the fact that the United States was now an infinitely more settled and prosperous nation, they sometimes yearned for the exciting days of their youth, when they could ride about, showing their enemies what they thought of them with shot and shell. One last, armed action in a righteous cause piqued the quixotic fancy of these older men. The youngsters sensed an opportunity to emulate their fathers and uncles and to go to war on those who would invade their territory. They, too, wished for a share of glory.

So it was that as Sheriff Tom Parker and his son

went round Mayfield that July day, they found themselves unwittingly tapping into deep longings and
hopes that were not at all evident on the surface of
the little town. All of which meant in plain terms
that when the sheriff sought a muster of those who
would ride alongside him the next day, he really
didn't need to fret about how he would find the five
dollars a day to pay the men. They would probably
have paid twice that amount out of their own
money, merely for the pleasure of fighting what
looked to all parties likely to be the last armed confrontation on such a scale as any of them would live
to see.

CHAPTER 7

The day of Jack Parker's sixteenth birthday, 18 July 1891, dawned bright and fair. His father wished him many happy days of the sort in the future, and presented him with a heavy parcel, wrapped up in brown paper and fastened with string and sealing wax. Not having expected anything in the way of a gift, other than being sworn in as a deputy, the boy opened the parcel and found a stout, pasteboard box. Within, on a bed of dried straw, lay a long-barrelled pistol. His father said, 'It's a single action army model, the artilleryman's version. You're no great shakes with a pistol, but this is as good as a rifle if you hold it right.' When Jack said nothing, his father said, 'You like it?'

'Pa, it's just beautiful. I don't need to pull the trigger to raise the hammer, is that right? That's what spoils my aim so often with pistols.'

'No, you just cock it so, with your thumb,' said Sheriff Parker, taking the gun from the box and suiting the action to the words, 'It only takes the gentlest pressure on the trigger and the hammer'll fall. Might help your aim some.'

Jack took the pistol from his father's hand and hefted it in his own. The balance felt just right and, as his father had observed, the long barrel looked a little like a rifle. He said, 'I don't have a holster, sir.'

'You can borrow a rig from the office. You'll need a dragoon holster for this, I'm sure we have such a one. It'll be no good for quick draws or any of that foolishness, you know. But with practice, I guess we can make you as good a shootist as the next man.'

After a substantial breakfast of pancakes, the two of them started out for the office. Even before they arrived, it was plain that something unusual was taking place. From afar, they could see a dozen or so mounted men, milling about the roadway and by the look of it, others were arriving. When they reached the sheriff's office, it became obvious by their clothing and demeanour that these were men from out of town, farmers who had abandoned their fields to come on an errand to town. What that errand was soon became apparent. Jerry Reece had been an effective emissary the previous day, for these men were effectually roused and wished to be sworn in as part of a legally constituted posse. Even as he established this by speaking to a few of them, the sheriff saw another three men ride up. If this continued, then there would be no need for anybody from the town itself to take part in the action which Sheriff Parker had planned.

A scene like this though, with grim-faced men, all well armed, mustering in the public highway like this, precipitated the men of Mayfield to action, lest they be left out of the game. Men on the way to open up their hardware stores, stopped in their tracks and, having discovered what was going on, hurried home to fetch their own weapons. Young hotheads begged the day off work from their employers, and they, too, fetched their scatterguns, hunting rifles and pistols, and congregated outside the sheriff's office. By ten that morning, the crowd numbered over a hundred, and the ordinary mercantile activity of the town had ground to a halt.

As noon approached, it seemed to Sheriff Parker that unless Mayfield were to descend wholly into chaos, he should get these men moving against the enemy. He advised that each man should acquire provisions for a day or two and that they would be moving off at one in the afternoon precisely. It appeared that the telegraph lines were still down and that it was accordingly impossible to communicate with Cheyenne. One of the homesteaders, though, had news of the invaders, who had stayed seemingly at Timothy Carter's ranch the previous night; camping out in and around his land. The rumour was that they had a list of seventy names of men who were alleged to be rustlers. The intention of the 'range detectives' was to call upon these men and either detain them, inflict summary justice or to draw them into gunfights, in which the odds would be overwhelmingly in favour of the Texans. Word was, that if nothing was done, then all the barbed wire fences of the settlers would be torn down over the next week or so, the soddies destroyed, the owners scattered to the four winds, and all the newly cultivated land returned to open range.

At one, the column of men left Mayfield. Women and children, along with older men, stopped still on the sidewalk to watch the procession. It looked precisely like what it was: a hastily assembled little army, going off to war. In total, there were well over two hundred and fifty men in the posse. Nothing like it had been seen since the war, almost thirty years before. However battle-hardened and heavily armed the southerners might be, they would be outnumbered by better than five to one if it came to a pitched battle.

At the head of the band rode Sheriff Parker, with his son. The other two deputies rode up and down the column, ensuring that stragglers kept up and that they all rode as a compact force. Although he could not allow it to be seen, Tom Parker was uneasily aware that his military experience was far from sufficient for such a task as this. During the war, he had from time to time found himself in charge of a patrol of a dozen or so men, but nothing on this scale. He had no real notion of tactics or military stratagems which might be useful when directing half a regiment or so on the battlefield. But then, he reflected privately, perhaps it would not actually come to combat. Seeing themselves so vastly outnumbered, Carter's hired bullies might decide to throw in their hands without a fight. Fervently as he hoped that this would be how the day would pan out, in his heart of hearts the sheriff did not for a moment believe that this would happen.

Jack was exulting in the possession of his new pistol. It hung now at his belt in the long, military holster that his father had rooted out for him. Capable as he was with a rifle, Jack had never really taken to shooting with a handgun. This weapon was different, though. With its long barrel and satisfying weight, he had an idea that once he had got the hang of the thing, he would soon be as handy with the single-action Colt as he was with the Winchester.

There was something indescribably thrilling, for a boy who had just that very day turned sixteen at any rate, in riding at the head of a large body of men intending to make a stand for what was right. Jack Parker had devoured any number of dime novels in which this very thing had been delineated in the purplest of prose, but the reality far outstripped anything he had read. But the excitement was tinged and leavened by the fear that he felt – not only the fear that he, Jack Parker, might take a wound or even die in the course of an armed affray, but, even worse, the dread that he would prove not to be up to the job. This was enough to make him flush hotly when he thought of it, the idea that if and when any shooting started, he would cut and run, shaming both himself and his father.

Jack would have been mortified if anybody had guessed what he was worrying about as they rode down on Timothy Carter's spread. Fortunately though, his face remained impassive. From time to time Sheriff Parker stole a sideways glance at his son and was pleased to note that the boy seemed as cool and collected as could be. He thought, once again, how alike his son was to himself at a similar age.

There was no sign of life at Carter's place. Not only did nobody seem to be about, there was little evidence, either, that above fifty men had lately been based here – no tents or other accommodation. Sheriff Parker guessed that they had merely bivouacked in the vicinity of Carter's house, and that the men were behaving now as though they were on active service in enemy territory, sleeping rough and without a permanent base until they had undertaken whatever commission they had been given by Carter and cronies in the WSGA. Was it true, as he had that morning been told, that a list of seventy names had been compiled and the aim was to rid the area of all those individuals? A swift calculation suggested that if each of the men on this supposed list was farming a section of a hundred and sixty acres, then disposing of them all would allow better than eleven thousand acres to be returned to open range. This would leave the remaining homesteaders to feel vulnerable and could be enough to trigger a general exodus.

While musing in this way, Sheriff Parker heard a rattle of metallic clicks as men around him raised their rifles and cocked them. He looked round to see what had promoted such a reaction, and saw, walking out of the barn, an old and decrepit man. It was Carter's night watchman, who was as ancient as Methuselah and reputed by the local youths to have taken part in the War of Independence the previous century. As soon as he saw the man, Sheriff Parker cried out urgently, 'Don't nobody fire! This man means no harm.' Then he called out to Dave Jenkins, 'What's afoot, old-timer? Where is everyone?'

'Danged if I know,' replied the old man querulously. 'They don't tell me nothing.'

'I hear there was a heap o' folk camped here last night.'

'Sure was. Big bunch of Southrons, but what they were about is more than I could say. They set off an hour since, heading east.'

'You know where they was headed?'

'Couldn't say. Up to mischief though, I'll be bound. They're that kind of men.'

'All right boys,' shouted the sheriff to the men behind him, 'We're going to speed up a bit and ride east, a good canter'd be the best dodge. That way, we might cross the path of those boys afore they've had time to cause more trouble.' To Dave Jenkins, Tom Parker said, 'Were I you, I'd get under cover and stay there. You'll find there's any number of trigger-happy fools about today.'

The track east led in the general direction of Scotts Bluff, but before that town was reached, there was a patchwork quilt of fields and little small-holdings which would one day, in the not-too-distant future, become settled, agricultural land. At present though, it was little better than frontier, part wild and part tamed and cultivated. At a guess, the Texans were going to shoot up a few places, kill one or two men and hope to stampede the rest into digging up and leaving their claims, before they had had a chance to prove up on them.

It was quite impossible for so many riders to proceed at a canter along the track and so, at a word of command from the sheriff, they spread out on to the grassy plain which lay upon either side of the road and rode on that as well. They were not charging yet at any enemy whom they could see and so there was no need for them to bunch up. The mass of riders scattered outwards, until there was at least six or ten feet between each horse.

About twenty minutes after leaving Timothy Carter's ranch, smoke was seen in the distance, trickling up into the clear blue sky. When they reached the source of it, they found it to be a wooden cabin, which was almost burnt out. There was no sign of whoever had been living there, but it could be seen that a tangle of barbed wire lay on the ground for some distance about, along with uprooted wooden posts. It seemed that the process of returning the land to open range was already in progress. 'Anybody know whose place this is?' asked Sheriff Parker. It appeared that nobody did.

As they moved on from the burnt out cabin, another cloud was soon ahead of them; over the crest of a low rise of ground. It was pale grey, not tinged with blue like woodsmoke. Jack said suddenly to his father, 'That's not smoke. It's dust being kicked up by horses or cattle.'

'Well spotted, son. I should just about say that you were right.'

When they reached the top of the high ground, they were able to see to the distant horizon. Some two or three miles off was a group of riders, kicking up the dust, which rose and hung in the still air like that pillar of smoke which Scripture says led Moses and the chosen people through the wilderness. It was too far to be able to distinguish individual figures, let alone count them, but there was no doubt that it was a sizeable number of riders. Sheriff Parker waited on the hilltop until others began to catch up with him. Then he yelled for them all to stop. It took a little time for his order to be passed from one man to the next and for a minute or two the whole posse was a chaotic mass of moving and shouting men. Eventually, things quietened down and the sheriff was able to make himself heard. He cried, 'That there is the men as are acting unlawfully. As members of a legally constituted posse, every one of you is indemnified against any claim against you arising from the execution of your duties. Even so, don't act hasty. We're going to pursue those men as fast as can be, but I don't want any shooting until I say the word. Is that clear? I'd as soon end this without bloodshed, if that's humanly possible.'

It seemed to Tom Parker that some of those on the far edge of the great crowd might not have heard his words and his heart misgave him. He surely did not wish to launch a war; merely to put a stop to the activities of the Wyoming Stock Growers' Association. He shouted even louder, saying, 'Recollect what I say. No firing unless I give the word.' Then he waved his arm and gestured that they were to make their way towards the pillar of dust hanging in the air a couple of miles away. At that point, everything began to unravel and Sheriff Parker saw that the best laid plans could be wrecked by so trifling a matter was the topography of a district.

The fifty or so riders had perhaps caught sight of the hundreds of men riding down on them. At any rate, they set off at a smart pace, heading east or from right to left according to the perspective of Sheriff Parker's posse. At a guess, thought the sheriff, they were not minded to try conclusions with a body of men perhaps four or five times as large as their own, and were making towards Timothy Carter's ranch to consider their tactics. It must have come as a shock to the marauders to find that there were plenty and enough men in this part of Wyoming who were prepared to stand up to them and meet force with force.

Most of the men in the posse were now galloping hell for leather to cut off the retreat of the Texans and offer battle. This would have been all well and good, except that a thickly wooded tongue of land lay between pursuers and their prey. Riding as they were to intercept the other men meant that Parker's posse was going straight towards this wood, when what they really ought to be doing was to head to the right, avoid the trees and then try and catch up the other riders by chasing after them. The point was that this stretch of woodland was as thick and dark as could be. It was a part of the great forest which had once covered this part of the land. So closely spaced were the trees and so tangled the shrubbery which grew around them, that even walking through that little forest was a trial. Riding through it at anything other than a slow walking pace would be quite impossible. The sheriff knew from the lay of the land that on their present course, his men would need to weave their way through a good half mile of forest and force a path through all the brush as well. It would take at least forty minutes for all the posse to make their way through there and emerge clear on the other side.

'Hey, you men!' shouted Sheriff Parker at the top of his voice. 'Wait up now. You need to go round that wood, not through it.' He might as well have called to the wind for all the notice that was taken of him. Many of the men riding in the posse were whooping and making noises suggestive of martial valour. None of them seemed in the least degree minded to listen to what their leader had to say. For a moment, the thought crossed Sheriff Parker's mind that firing a couple of shots in the air would gain their attention, but he soon abandoned this scheme as being excessively reckless. The mood those boys were in, they'd like as not start firing at random if they suspicioned that an enemy was shooting near or by them. Parker had seen just that very thing happen during the war.

'Jack!' called the sheriff, 'Hold up there. Rein in.' His son stopped and the mass of men rode on heedlessly. 'I'd o' thought that those blamed deputies of mine would have had more sense,' muttered Tom Parker, as a couple of hundred men careered headlong down the slope towards the wood, 'Looks like they lost their heads too.'

Nobody seemed to have noticed the absence of their nominal leader, as the posse reached the trees and began forcing a passage through the wood. 'What should we do, Pa?' asked Jack, 'Ride round the wood or just make straight off now towards Mr Carter's place. That's if you think they're headed there.'

'They're on their way to Carter's ranch, for a bet. This has taken them aback a little, I'm thinking. They thought they'd have a clear run at whatever villainy they got in mind. If nothing else, we queered their pitch a little and set them off balance. That's a good beginning.'

130

'So what's to do?'

'I reckon as we'll take the long route, round the wood. Happen we'll be able to meet the rest of that crew as they come out the other side. Damn fools.'

The father and son set off down the hill at a lively trot and when once they had gained the level ground at the bottom, they spurred on their horses; at first into a canter and then a gallop. It took twenty minutes to work their way round the wood and onto the track which led east, in the general direction of Timothy Carter's ranch. Jack was congratulating himself on having had the good sense to mark what his father was about, rather than just tailing after the others. He guessed that Pa would have a few choice words for his two regular deputies for their impetuous behaviour.

Riding along the edge of the wood, both the sheriff and his son kept their ears cocked for any sound of movement in the trees, such as would indicate that the posse was almost through. Although the men had made enough noise to raise Cain when they were charging down that slope, the effort of struggling through the thick undergrowth must have quietened them down a bit. Jack and his father had to cool their heels for the best part of a quarter-hour before they began to hear the sound of men cursing and complaining. It was another fifteen minutes before the first of the men of the posse struggled free of the toils and emerged from the wood, greeting the sheriff shamefacedly.

Slowly, the men whom Sheriff Parker hoped would help him to restore order in Benton County straggled from the thick undergrowth and assembled in the roadway. The two deputies attempted some slight apology to their boss when they finally got free of the tangled woodland, but by that time Tom Parker was beyond being annoyed and simply waved off their expressions of regret, too weary even to reproach the men for their stupidity.

When everybody seemed to have made it through, the sheriff addressed them thus: 'I'm guessing that you all know that those blackguards will have had time by now to make themselves comfortable at Carter's place? Most likely they've set up defensible positions and prepared for our arrival. Had you men just waited a second and listened to me, we'd have caught them on the hop, run them down before they even reached the ranch. Well, there it is. This foolishness has made the business ten times more difficult and a sight more dangerous than it might otherwise have been – and that's all I have to say on the subject.'

It was a subdued and chastened bunch of men who set off down the road at a trot. There was little enough point in galloping after their quarry now. As the sheriff had correctly pointed out, they would not now be able to overtake the men they were hunting in the open. Chances were that they would be hunkered down at Timothy Carter's ranch, ready and waiting for the approach of the sheriff's men.

Dealing with fifty men who were dug in and ready to defend their positions was a horse of another colour entirely from an equal battle in the open between opposing groups of riders.

'What will we do?' asked Jack curiously of his father, 'Meaning if they won't surrender to you?'

'Surrender?' said Sheriff Parker in surprise, the idea not having previously occurred to him. 'Those boys won't surrender. Why should they? There's murder been done and they'll none of them be keen to lay down their weapons and allow themselves to be hanged.'

'You wouldn't hang 'em, Pa, would you? Not without a trial and all?'

'I wouldn't, but they're not to know that. Fools. You never seen the Bible text, where it says that, "The wicked flee where none pursueth?"'

'Then what?'

Tom Parker lowered his voice, so that only his son could hear what he was saying. 'Truth is, boy, I don't rightly know what's going to happen next. I saw one or two sieges during the war, but encountering such a thing in civil life will be something of a novelty.'

Just exactly as they feared, by the time the ranch came in sight it was plain that this was going to be no easy enterprise. While they had only been riding against individual homesteads, with just one or two men to deal with, the Texans had been fearless and bold enough. Now, faced with a couple of hundred armed men whose blood was up, the case was altered and the invaders showed no inclination to fight. Instead, they were seemingly determined to stay put and await further developments. When the first riders of the posse came within a hundred yards of Carter's house, a couple of shots rang out. Nobody was hurt; in all probability this was meant to be a warning, and whoever fired was like as not shooting wide on purpose. The message, though, was clear: keep back, or there will be bloodshed.

Over half the men in Sheriff Parker's posse were veterans of the war between the states, and these men knew that there is one infallible rule of warfare, from the time of the ancient Romans, right up to the present day: that the advantage always lies with the defender. Those hiding behind walls or crouched in ditches, able to steady their weapons and take careful aim, are always better situated than men running towards them across open ground. It was so at Agincourt and Crecy, and it is as true in the age of repeating rifles.

After those warning shots had been fired, Sheriff Parker called for his column to halt and began to consider well what his next course of action should be. It was while he was pondering on this important question that there was another shot from the direction of Timothy Carter's place and a ball struck Tom Parker on the side of his head and sent him tumbling from his horse.

CHAPTER 8

When he saw his father fall from the horse upon which he was mounted, it seemed to Jack Parker that his heart stopped beating momentarily. He could not breathe and felt as panicky as a girl. This passed in an instant and he leapt from his own horse and rushed over to where his father lay still in the dust of the track. Brandon Ross and Jerry also jumped down and came over to see what was to do. Jerry said, 'Is he breathing?'

'He's breathing,' said Jack, 'Thank the Lord, I don't think he's badly hurt. The ball must've just grazed his head here at the side. Look!'

Sheriff Parker's temple was indeed grazed, but it was plain that no bullet had entered, nor shattered, his skull. He was breathing as peacefully as a man slumbering in his bed at night, quite oblivious to what was going on around him. Jack said to the deputies, 'Help me to move him to the side, so's he won't get trampled on by all them riders.' Once this was done, he said to Brandon Ross and Jerry Reece, 'Well, I guess it's up to us, leastways 'til my pa comes to.'

The idea of acting without instructions or even the authority of their boss seemed to be a strange and unwelcome one to the two young men. Brandon said, 'We best not take any action for now. Tom, which is to say your father, is apt to get mighty irritated if'n me and Jerry does stuff off our own bat, as they say.' Jerry Reece nodded his agreement and muttered, 'Ain't that the truth!'

Looking from one man to the other, Jack saw to his amazement that neither deputy was willing to take any responsibility for what was to be done. One thing seemed to him quite certain, and that was that it would be crazy-mad to leave the men of the posse to their own devices. There would be shooting and bloodshed and who knew what, and all to no purpose. Somebody needed to arrange things so that those wretches, now holed up in and around Mr Carter's house, did not either escape or launch a sudden and unexpected attack on those who had pursued them. Keenly aware that he was the youngest present and being most unwilling to push his self forward, the boy said to both Brandon and Jerry, 'I'll take any blame attached to it, but we got to do something. When my father comes to, you can tell him it was all my doing, but we must get some of the men to work round the outside of the yard and barn and take up positions in the shelter of those trees. Else, some of those fellows from Texas might try and circle round us and come at us from the rear.'

Having been absolved from responsibility and seeing that Jack was willing to shoulder responsibility should the plan miscarry, the two young deputies did as he had suggested and sent two dozen men to make their way around Carter's home and yard, so that they could take up posts on the other side of the property and give warning if any of the Texans looked likely to spring a surprise attack.

Jack checked his father once more and was reassured to find that he was still unconscious and breathing easily. Had he not known what had happened, the sheriff's son would have thought that his pa had taken it into his head to lay down and have a refreshing sleep. Brandon and Jerry came over to see how their boss was doing. Brandon said, 'Well, we got some of the boys to make their way round the back there. Anybody tries to escape that way, we got them covered. Other than that, I don't see there's much to be done.'

'We could move the most of the men back, out of range of anybody minded to start firing on us,' said Jack hesitantly. 'We'd set some of those with muskets to set a watch on this side as well. Maybe conceal themselves and keep an eye on things. Then we could see what was needful to be done next.'

Coming to, Sheriff Parker became aware of a

man giving instructions relating to the disposition of forces taking part in some kind of action. For a second or two, Tom Parker did not know where he was or what had happened, and wondered if he was dreaming of the war, as he sometimes did. Then he suddenly knew exactly where he was, and realized to his utter amazement that the quietly confident man he had heard giving orders was none other than his own son. The thought stunned him, and for that fraction of an instant he was privileged to be able to see his own child through other people's eyes. Instead of a callow youth, he heard a young man with an air of leadership about him, somebody to whom others listened and of whom they took notice. It was a most disconcerting revelation to see his son at a distance, as it were.

The sheriff got to his feet and said, 'Who's in charge of this expedition son, you or me?'

Turning round sharply, Jack's face lit up at the sight of his father restored to his usual vigour. He said apologetically, 'I'm sorry sir, I didn't mean to step in where I wasn't needed.'

A warm smile spread across his father's face, not at all a common thing for the sheriff, and he said quietly, 'You've nothing to say sorry for. You're doing just fine.'

'Are you sure that you're all right, boss?' asked Jerry Reece. 'Shouldn't you stay sitting for a spell, case you get giddy or aught like that?'

'Stop fussing, man,' said Sheriff Parker. 'You're

138

worse than a woman. You have those boys penned up nice and secure, I hope?'

It appeared that Tom Parker was none the worse for the glancing blow that the musket ball had caught him, and he swiftly took command again. The blow to his head had not shaken him overly much, and his mind was now made up about the course of action which he and the others would be taking. If those Texan invaders wanted a fight, then they could have it. As far as the sheriff was concerned, he would be happy to see every man-Jack of the southrons killed in battle, if that was what it would take to rid Benton County of them. Like his son, he could not forget nor forgive the lynching of a woman, and if these men thought that they could usurp authority and deal out death as they pleased, then he, Sheriff Tom Parker, was the one to show them the error of their ways.

The plan that Sheriff Parker had come up with was a simple enough one. Most of the men from the posse were now stationed around Carter's house, barn and fields, where the 'range detectives' were, although they couldn't be seen. The only way that they would be leaving that area was either in pine boxes or by surrendering and yielding up their arms. It was not in reason to expect the posse to settle down for a protracted siege, and so if there was no sign of surrender within the next twenty-four hours or by dusk the following day, then the sheriff intended to storm the ranch and kill anybody who offered resistance. In the meantime, he kept enough men positioned around the area where the Texans were, to be sure of knowing if any attempt were made to break out. The main body of his men, over a hundred strong, he held back in reserve. These would be the ones who would carry out the attack on the ranch house and barn the next day.

It was now about two or three in the afternoon, and if these plans were adhered to, thought Jack, then there was likely to be great loss of life the next day. The thought troubled him, angry and bitter as he still was about the murder of Aggie Roberts. Even now, he did not understand the full import of what was afoot. It was not until he came across his father talking in a low voice to Brandon Ross that Jack fully collected what was being planned. Perhaps being knocked out in the way that he had been by that musket-ball had enraged his father and clouded his judgement, or perhaps it was what he had intended all along; Jack had no idea. But as he approached his father, where he was speaking to the deputy of his plans for the following day, he distinctly heard the sheriff say, 'I don't look for them to surrender. We'll kill every mother's son of those rogues tomorrow, I'm telling you.' It was the first intimation that a massacre was being planned and that his own father was the instigator of it.

On hearing these words, Jack Parker slipped away, without speaking to his father. He needed to do some serious thinking. He walked around a little, reasoning the matter out to his own satisfaction. One point, which should have been perfectly obvious, now struck him, and he resolved to check this at once with his father. He went back to where he had last seen his father, but could find neither the sheriff nor Brandon Ross. When he did track them down, it was to find a conversation going on between his father and his deputies and a half-dozen other men. Chary of pushing himself forward, Jack stood on the edge of the little group, somewhat to the back of his father, so he was out of sight. What he heard horrified him beyond measure.

Tom Parker said, 'It might be time to poke the anthill a little, stir things up, you know.'

'Meaning what, sheriff? In practical terms?' replied a man whom Jack did not know, but who looked as though he was probably a settler. 'You mean get them men riled up a little?'

'I was thinking of firing on them a little and see how they like the experience,' said Sheriff Parker, 'Wouldn't like 'em to feel too comfortable and secure in there, you know.'

'You think that might get them to think about surrender?' asked Jerry Reece. 'If they know they're outnumbered, that is?'

'Surrender, nothing!' growled Jack's father, 'Time's passed for such. I aim to show those fellows who's running the show around here. When we're through, it'll be the end of the WSGA and all those

141

bastards away over in Cheyenne.'

There were murmurs of approval to these words, and then Jack said loudly the question which had struck him only a few minutes before, 'Do those men in Mr Carter's place know that this is a legal posse, led by the sheriff?'

The men turned and stared at him, which prompted Jack to explain further. 'What I mean is, they might just think that this is an armed band of homesteaders and such. If they was to be told that the sheriff is here and the whole thing legal, then they might give up. If they knew that we'd spare their lives, that is.'

These sensible remarks of the young man were met with complete silence. Then his father said, 'Jack, you done right well today and I'll be the first to own it, but this is a deal more complicated than you know. Whyn't you head over and see if those men around the perimeter need anything doing for them?'

Despite the fact that he was actually wearing a star, Jack felt that he was being treated humiliatingly like a little boy who had been interrupting the adults' business and was now being sent off on a chore to get him out of the way. He wandered disconsolately round the outposts, trying to make out the play. There was still no sign of anybody in Carter's place. Presumably they were all sheltering in the house and barn.

It was not until his perambulations had described

almost a complete circuit of the ranch-house and associated buildings that Jack found out how matters really stood. Until that moment, he had persuaded himself that he might be mistaken about the plans which his father and the others had for the men they had surrounded. At first, he thought that the whole fraught situation was about to end in the best way imaginable, for a man waved a white cloth from one of the upper windows of the big house. It was the clearest indication possible that a truce was required; who knew, perhaps even an unconditional surrender was contemplated?

The youngster was nearing the group of men containing his father, who were still evidently continuing their discussions. These men had seen the waving of the white flag, and since so many of them were former combatants in the war, there could be little doubt that they would recognize the significance of the action on the part of an enemy. Then as he watched, Jack Parker saw his father do something which shocked him to his very core. He said something which Jack didn't hear to one of those standing nearby, and in response, the man handed him a rifle. Sheriff Parker took it and worked the lever, cocking the piece and bringing a cartridge into the breech. Then he raised the weapon and fired straight at the window from which the white flag was being flown.

A short period of dead silence followed the shot, before some of the men in the house replied with a desultory crackle of musketry. They were perhaps as surprised as Jack at this open contempt for the rules of civilised warfare. He heard his father yell, 'All right boys, let them have it!' and there began a vigorous storm of shooting from the men surrounding the house.

Jack threw himself to the ground when the firing began, not wishing to make himself an easy target, but after no more than ten seconds, the exchange of fire petered out and silence reigned once more. Even though it was now safe again, the young man remained laying where he was. His mind was working furiously and he had no desire to speak to anybody, which might have disturbed the train of his thoughts.

It was as plain as day to Jack Parker that there was more about this business than he rightly understood. Indeed, his father had hinted as much to him when he sent him off on that snipe hunt of making the rounds of the sentries. What it might be, the youngster could hardly guess. Something about bringing down Timothy Carter and the Wyoming Stock Gowers Association, perhaps? There was no doubt that his father was no admirer of Carter and his outfit. Then again, there was some friction between the sheriff and the mayor. Did that have any bearing on things? Ultimately, Sheriff Parker was employed by the town of Mayfield and the mayor was the leading citizen there. Was his father hoping to see the mayor out of his position?

144

Whatever was going on, it was obvious that the men defending the Carter place were doomed. Jack's father had shown what he thought of any surrender, and it looked as though he was intent upon killing all those whom he held penned up, probably including Mr Carter himself. It was not to be thought of that he, Jack Parker, could either countenance such a massacre nor refrain from doing everything humanly possible to prevent its taking place. There was no point in reasoning with his father, he could see that, but something must be done to stop this terrible thing from taking place.

In the back of Jack's mind, something was stirring, something which might aid him in this endeavour. He had been compelled at school recently to study the constitution of the United States, and also some of the amendments and alterations made to the constitution since the war which had ended in 1865. He racked his brains and then realized that the information he sought would surely be found in the law books which his father kept in his office. The young man's frame gave an involuntary shudder at the thought of actually entering the sheriff's office uninvited and making free with what was found there. It would certainly jeopardize the newly found and precious cordiality which currently existed between he and his father, but when it came right down to it, a body had to do what he knew to be right. However wickedly some of the men trapped in that ranch house had behaved, he could not stand back and see them all killed out of hand, which was what was like to happen tomorrow afternoon, unless he took some action.

There would be little purpose in slipping away from the scene of what was, in effect, a siege, until it became dark and nobody would be able to see what he was about. Trying to gallop off towards town in broad daylight would be madness. All he needed to do was to conceal his real feelings regarding what was happening here and then as soon as night fell, he could make off towards Mayfield. Jack hated the idea of betraying his father and was even more grieved at the disappointment which his father would feel towards his son, but there it was. If nothing else, he was likely to save his father from becoming a murderer; although he doubted that the sheriff would see the thing in that light.

Sheriff Parker was busy as evening came, ensuring that the men posted around the ranch were careful not to allow anybody to escape. As he put it, 'We need to keep all the rats in one trap!' So busy was he with such matters, that he actually forgot about his son and altogether failed to notice until much later, by which time Jack had led his mount away in the darkness. Once he had walked the mare a good distance, he saddled up and rode as fast as he dared in the dark, along the track leading to town.

It was approaching eleven by the time that Jack reached Mayfield and most folk were in their beds. Certainly, nobody took the least notice of the boy as

146

he looped the horse's reins over the hitching post outside the office and opened the door with the keys with which his father had entrusted him. He didn't reckon that anybody would be minded to trouble at this time of night if they saw a light in the office and in any case, he was a real deputy now and so had a perfect right to be there at any hour of the day or night that he chose. He accordingly rummaged in one of the drawers of the desk, found a box of Lucifers and lit a lamp. Having done this, he went over to the shelf of books and selected one which he felt was likely to provide him with the necessary information.

Finding the relevant law was easy enough, but now Jack Parker came to the real matter and, finding that this was where the knife met the bone, he was scared and worried that he might be about to do the wrong thing. That the action which he contemplated was criminal, he knew. That all that stemmed from it would be fraud and deception, he likewise knew. That was neither here nor there, though, not if he was actually saving lives and stopping his own father from doing a dreadful and wicked thing. He knew where his father kept the notepaper with the official heading of his office, and went to fetch a couple of sheets.

Sitting at his father's desk with the lawbook in front of him, so that he could use the correct expressions, Jack Parker composed the following letter:

To Officer Commanding, Fort McKinley
July 18th 1891

Sir,

I, Sheriff Thomas Parker, am the only lawful representative of the Civil Power in the town of Mayfield, State of Wyoming. A band of armed, irregular Forces have arrived in this area and begun to commit various acts of warfare, including Murder, mayhem, looting and rapine. Various individuals have been deprived of their civil rights by being hanged or shot to death.

Under the powers invested in the Federal Army by the Enforcement Acts of 1870 and 1871, I call upon you to provide urgent aid and assistance to suppress this rebellion.

I have the honour to remain, sir,

Your Obedient Servant, Thomas Parker (Sheriff).

Having completed this missive, with many crossings out and alterations, Jack copied it out in a fair hand and then placed it in an envelope addressed to the commanding officer of Fort McKinley. It was a fearful thing to forge his own father's signature in this way, to say nothing of misleading the army, but he didn't see that he had another choice.

After tucking the letter inside his jacket, the young man extinguished the lamp and left the office, locking the door behind him. Then he mounted up and headed out of town, due east, towards Fort McKinley. He reckoned that taking an easy pace in the darkness, for fear of laming the mare, he was likely to reach the army base a little before dawn. Allowing that they took this letter seriously and set off almost at once, they should be in plenty of time to save those men trapped at Mr Carter's place.

The ride to Fort McKinley was uneventful but exceedingly slow and tedious. Jack dared not ride any faster than a brisk trot. The lives of fifty men or more depended upon him, and if his horse took a tumble in the darkness, then he would never get word to the army in time. The only bit of excitement came when he was nearly shot as he approached the fort, just as the first glimmer of dawn touched the sky in the east.

As the silhouette of the wooden stockade walls became visible ahead, there was a sharp, metallic sound nearby and a hoarse voice cried, 'Stand to! Who are ye and what's your business?'

Figuring, quite correctly, that a musket aiming in his direction had just been cocked, Jack reined in and said, 'I'm a deputy sheriff. I have an urgent communication for your commanding officer.'

'Don't go making any sudden movements, 'cause any mistake I make ain't like to be set right in this world,' said the sentry who had challenged him, 'Just set still and I'll approach.' Having done so, the fellow struck a light and peered up at Jack, noting the star on his jacket. He said, 'You look powerful young for a deputy. You sure this ain't some game?'

'Not a bit of it. This is life and death.'

'Well then, you'd best proceed. Holler up when you reach the gate.' Having delivered himself of this advice, the man melted back into the shadows.

It took some little while to persuade the sergeant who first spoke to Jack Parker about his business that this was a matter which needed to be brought at once to his officer's attention, but when once that august personage was awakened and had read the letter, he swung into action immediately. In no time at all, a bugle was rousing the fort and a troop of men snatched a hurried breakfast before swinging themselves into the saddle. Captain Tregarth had looked a mite dubiously at Jack Parker, observing that this 'deputy' was not even of an age to shave, but there was no gainsaying the appeal for military assistance, which was couched in precise and legal terms. On the off-chance though that it turned out to be some elaborate hoax, the captain said, 'You'll be riding with us, Deputy Parker. If nothing else, we'll need to be guided to this place.' If it was a mare's nest, then Captain Tregarth purposed to have the perpetrator alongside him, so that he could find out what the game was.

The thought of meeting his father in the

company of a column of cavalry whom he had summoned by the false use of his name was not an enticing one to Jack, but he didn't see that he had another choice. He said, 'Of course, sir.'

The raising of what later became known as 'the siege of Carter's ranch' was anticlimactic in the extreme. The cavalry reached the ridge above Timothy Carter's ranch an hour or so before midday and announced their arrival by a loud bugle call, with the aim of warning anybody in the vicinity that things were now changed and that the army were there to take charge.

The look on his father's face when he glimpsed Jack riding among the cavalry would stay with Jack Parker for a very long time. Sheriff Parker's mouth quite literally gaped open in a way that he had always told his son was uncouth. The worst moment for Jack came when Captain Tregarth asked where Sheriff Parker was and then proceeded to bring out the letter which had supposedly been sent, appealing for help from the military. This was when the sheriff could have disavowed his signature, with who knew what consequences for his son. Instead, he stared at the letter in the captain's hand with no discernible expression and then thanked him for responding so promptly. After that, it was just a question of allowing the cavalry to disarm the men holed up in the ranch house and barn.

There was not a little murmuring among the homesteaders who made up much of the posse.

151

These men had hoped to settle scores with Carter and his 'range detectives', especially Dave Booker, who was generally felt to be the driving force behind the recent murders. There was nothing to be done, though, for Sheriff Parker had at once conceded that the cavalry had more authority than he himself in the matter. At least, though, the threat to their lives was now removed, as all the Texans had been rounded up and were now bound for Fort McKinley, along with Timothy Carter himself. Carter blustered and bluffed about what an important man he was, and how the governor would certainly hear about this humiliating episode, but none of his words had an effect upon Captain Tregarth, who merely said, 'This comes under military jurisdiction. We are acting in support of the civil power, and from what I've seen, there's something close enough to an invasion of this district happened. I'm more than half minded to declare a state of emergency and impose martial law.' That shut Carter up pretty sharpish.

Tom Parker stayed around the ranch long enough to see that everybody dispersed and that nobody had any thoughts about looting the place, now that the hated owner had been removed. When just he, Jack and the two deputies were left, the sheriff said, 'You boys can get off to your homes now. I guess we're about done for the day. Mind you're in all the earlier tomorrow, though!'

At last, the dreaded time arrived when Jack and

his father were left alone. Nothing was said for a spell and then Sheriff Parker said, in a more reasonable voice than his son thought he had any cause to expect, 'Mind explaining all this to me, son?'

Haltingly, the boy set out his reasons for acting as he had done. He laid particular emphasis on the horror he had felt at the idea of his own father carrying out what amounted to a cold-blooded massacre. When he had finished, his father said nothing, and then, to Jack's amazement, smiled. 'Well I'm damned,' said Tom Parker ruefully. 'I never expected to see the day when my own son sat in judgement on me. But you're in the right, Jack, and I'm wrong. I ain't ashamed to own it.'

'You're not mad at me?'

'Maybe I should be, but no, I ain't mad at you. You saw what you thought was right, and went ahead and did it, and to the Devil with the consequences. That's how a man should behave. Means I did something right with the raising of you.'

Relief flooded through Jack's body so readily that he felt, to his embarrassment, the sudden and urgent need to make water. He said to his father, 'Pa, I need to answer a call of nature.'

'You go right ahead. I'm going down yonder, to make sure that Carter's house is secured. I don't think anybody would try and make off with his goods and chattels, but you never can tell.'

As his father made his way on foot, down the

153

slope to the big house, Jack Parker slipped into the bushes to ease his bladder. It was while standing there that he became aware of an angry voice in the distance and when he had finished his business he went back through the undergrowth and saw that his father was standing with his hands raised, and that Dave Booker, the head of the range detectives, was covering him with a drawn pistol.

CHAPTER 9

Straining his ears, Jack Parker heard the southerner say, apparently in response to a question from his father, 'Down in the root cellar.' It wasn't hard to work out that Booker was explaining where he had been hiding and how he had escaped being rounded up with the others who had been taken away by the army. Moving very slowly, so that Booker would not catch sight of him on the edge of his field of vision, Jack dropped to his knees and crawled slowly over to where the mare was standing patiently. Keeping his eye on the scene below him, he reached up slowly and slid the Winchester from where it nestled in its scabbard at the front of the saddle. Then the young man lay down and tried to gauge the distance to the two men standing by the door of Timothy Carter's house.

By listening hard, Jack could pick up scraps of the conversation, which he judged to be taking place fifty yards away. As he tried to hear what was being said, Jack worked the lever, cocking the piece and bringing a cartridge into the chamber. He would only have one chance for this, and he had to be right on the spot with that first shot.

' . . . really screwed things up for us. . . .' said the Texan in a loud and harsh voice. 'Somebody'll pay.'

'Can't be helped,' said Tom Parker, 'Best you can do is just ride on out. I'll give you a fair start. . . .'

Squinting down the barrel of the rifle, the sheriff's son centred the sight on Dave Booker's ear. There could be no foolishness about 'winging' the man. If he was merely wounded, then there was every chance that he would still get off a shot at the man standing in front of him. Then again, even if he was shot right through the head, there was the possibility that his hand would contract in his death agonies and he would fire that pistol anyway.

' . . . you intend to do?'

'What d'you think, Parker? You're a dead man.'

There was no point in thinking this over now, because if he did that then he might not even be able to bring himself to fire. The thought of killing a man made Jack feel sick inside, but this was apt to be the only way of saving his father's life. He heard his father say loudly in a voice which was utterly lacking in fear or any other recognisable emotion, 'You best do what you will then.'

'Kneel down and I might let you live,' said Booker. 'Go on, on your knees!'

'I don't think it for a moment. You going to kill

156

me, just do it.'

And then time ran out and Jack knew that if he didn't act right at that point, then his father would be killed. Keeping the bead centred on Booker's head, the boy called out as loud as he could, 'Booker!'

The reaction from the range detective was as swift as a striking rattlesnake. He began turning towards Jack and raising the pistol to aim as he did so. Whereupon Jack Parker squeezed the Winchester's trigger and saw the man's head snap sharply back as the ball hit him straight through his forehead. Just as Jack had expected, the shock of being shot made the other man's hands twitch convulsively and the pistol went off with a sharp crack, which echoed back and forth like rolling thunder.

Sheriff Parker's reaction was almost as fast as Booker's had been, for as soon as Jack fired, his father went for his own pistol and let fly two shots at the man who had been holding him at gunpoint. Assured that his father was safe and had not been harmed, Jack got to his feet, found his legs a little unsteady, and then wondered why the horizon was swaying, as though he were on board a ship at sea. Following which, he fell to the ground in a dead faint.

When he came to, Jack found that his father was cradling his head in his lap and gazing down at him lovingly. Embarrassed at having passed out, and hoping that his father would not think it an unmanly proceeding, the boy tried to spring to his feet. The sheriff restrained his son, saying, 'Hush now, boy. You rest there.'

'I don't know what happened, I just came over unwell. . . .'

'What happened was that you saved my life, son, and I'm deeply sensible of it. That was a fair bit of marksmanship there.'

'He's dead? Booker, I mean?'

'Dead as a doornail,' replied his father cheerfully, 'I put a couple of balls in him as well, but that was to no purpose. You took him straight through his skull, he was dead before he hit the ground, I reckon.'

'Can we go home now? I feel better.'

During the ride back to Mayfield, neither Sheriff Parker nor his son had much to say. For Tom Parker, death had come close to claiming him that day, and even a hardened lawman such as he felt a little thoughtful about this. He had been sure that he was about to breathe his last. Jack's feelings were very different. He was mightily glad that he had been able to save his father's life, but the enormity of what he had done threatened to overwhelm him. He had a vivid recollection of the first time that he met Booker, which meant that the man had not been a stranger to him. He had been a living, breathing human, and now he was no more. To snuff out the life of a fellow being was an awe-inspiring thing to have done, and the youngster doubted that he would ever recover from the experience.

As they neared town, Sheriff Parker reined in his horse and said solemnly, 'You saved my life this day, and I'll not forget it. You want to work properly as a deputy, you surely earned the right. Hell, we make a good team. You've a conscience and a mind of your own too, which is not a bad thing. What do you say, son? That what you want?'

Before today, nothing would have thrilled Jack more than to hear such words from his father. But a killing can change everything. He said slowly, 'Truth to tell, sir, I don't think I'm cut out for this, not nohow. I killed a man. I don't ever aim to do such a thing again, not so long as I live.'

Jack's father eyed him thoughtfully, and at length said, 'What would you have, then?'

'I reckon college'd suit me better, sir. I'm sorry to disappoint you. . . .'

'You could never disappoint me, son. You've the makings of a fine man. For what it's worth, I'd say you're making the right choice. Some can shoot a man down and then carry on and do the same thing again, if it's needful. Others, you're one, only kill but once and then only when there's no other choice.' Tom Parker looked a little regretful though, and finished by saying, 'Mind, it's a crying shame. We would have made the hell of a team. Parker and son, lawmen to Benton County. Got a ring to it, wouldn't you say?' Then he laughed and spurred on his mount.

159

Even years later, when he became first a lawyer and, in later life, a judge, Jack Parker was never able to work out the truth of all that had happened in those few weeks in the summer of 1891. Pressure was brought to bear by the governor in Cheyenne, which led to the release of not only Timothy Carter, but all the southerners whom he had recruited as mercenaries. Once freed, the Texans had all headed straight back to their own territory, mindful that they had come within a whisker of being either lynched or brought before a regular court on a capital charge.

As for his father's aims and intentions in the matter, Jack never did learn why Mayfield's sheriff was so keen to massacre all those men. The mayor gave up his position shortly afterwards, and a friend of Tom Parker's was appointed to the job. The Wyoming Stock Growers Association folded up a short while later, but how that was connected with the events that July, Jack couldn't work out either.

One thing about which Jack Parker did not have any doubts or uncertainties, even in old age, was that those exciting days in July 1891 were when he ceased to be a boy and became a man, if not overnight, then certainly within the space of a few weeks.